I0623809

Tales from the CANYONS of the DAMNED

DANIEL ARTHUR SMITH

Tales from the Canyons of the Damned No. 13

First Edition

Special thanks to Jessica West and Chris Pourteau

ISBN-13: 978-1946777003 ISBN-10: 1946777005

~*~

For Susan, Tristan, & Oliver, as all things are.

~*~

Swipe Right

S. Elliot Brandis

~*~

The face staring at me from my smart phone is perfect. He has white teeth, a nice smile, and cheerful eyes. Behind him is a beach, the waves so crisp and immaculate they might as well be from a Pixar film. Only it's his life. David's life. His first name is right there in front of me, below his tanned chest.

I swipe left.

He's not what I'm looking for. I don't want perfect. I want ugly. Not in the physical way. I'm not a precious little monster. But I am a monster. I want to find the sick minded, the misogynistic. I want sexual predators. Self-proclaimed 'red pillers'. Game players.

Fucking assholes.

I dismiss a few more reasonable looking guys before somebody catches my eye. It's a selfie, taken in front of a mirror. His thumbs are tucked into the waist band of his jocks. Arm muscles bulge out from his white singlet. A wife beater. The singlet, that is. His profile says he's single. Looking for women who are 'DTF'. Down to fuck.

He's perfect. A different kind of perfect. Perfectly ugly.

I swipe right.

I send the first message. Douchebags love it when you send the first message. It makes you look desperate. I want him to think I'm desperate.

<You must hit the gym twice a day.> I type, slipping in a winking emoji for good measure.

He waits an hour before replying. This is deliberate. Again, it's a power game for guys like this. They want you to beg. They want to be in charge.

<If I'm taking it easy.> Kane says.

Yep, he even has an asshole name.

Now it's my turn to wait. He's talked himself up, now he's going to follow it up with a 'neg'. If you don't know what that means, I envy you. The 'neg' comes from negative, but it's really just an insult. This is part of the game. They say something jokey–almost innocent–that hurts you a little. *You look tired. Time to touch up those roots, hey? Wow, pretty brave of you to wear something like that! No offence.*

They never intend offence.

Except that's exactly the fucking point.

They want to knock you down as part of the power tussle. To build themselves up and make you work for it. To make you want to prove yourself. Basically, to make you even more desperate.

I'm explaining, not defending. These people are scum.

He replies right on schedule: <New phone?>

Weird angle. I won't lie—he's stumped me.

I reply: <No. Why?>

<Oh. Don't worry. Just a hunch.>

<Tell me.>

<It's just your photo. You have bags under your eyes. I figured it was a new phone, otherwise you'd have a better shot to put up. Something younger. No offense!>

Yeah, none taken. This guy is fucking perfect.

<Oh, you know.> I reply. <I like to party hard. I don't deny it. We call those morning after eyes.>

<You'll have more than morning after eyes when I'm done with you.>

<Is that right?>

<Yeah, baby.>

<What you doing tomorrow.>

<Hitting the club. But seriously, I'm not into time wasters. DTF or FO, know what I'm saying?>

<Don't worry, I'm a freak.>

Which, to be fair, isn't wrong. We set up a date. We'll catch up for a drink at a well know spot, down in the bowels of the clubbing district. It's not really a drink. It's more of an interview. A chance for him to see that I'm not a dog before he lures me back to his place, plies me with alcohol and drugs, and has 'consensual' sex with me. As consensual as it can be after the woman has become detached from reality. He will record the whole thing. Not on a video camera, but on his phone. These guys use phone apps to record audio from their encounters for use in court should she ever scream rape.

They are professional predators.

Without a doubt.

I'm okay with that.

I am a predator, too.

~*~

"You Mae?" Kane asks.

He actually looks creepily like his Tinder pic. Minus the wife beater, that is. In its place is a tight button up shirt, a sort of weird teal colour. The thin material is stretched over his body, showing the pattern of bad tattoos under his chest. I think I see a girl, fingering her tattooed self. Classy stuff.

"Yeah," I say. "Kane?"

"My mates call me The Weapon."

"Yeah, I won't be calling you that."

"Fine. Want a drink."

"Vodka and cranberry."

He smiles. That's the right answer. Hard spirits, but with a trashy twist. No offense if you like cranberry. It tastes pretty nice. Y'know, after they smother those bitter sons of bitches with sugar.

"Yo, Pete." He seems to know the bartender. That's a good sign for me, but a bad sign in general. "Get me a Jack and Coke. Oh, and a double vodka cranberry for the lady."

"Sure thing."

Pete looks me up and down. Or: Up, down, up, down, hover. The hover is near my breasts. It lasts a long time. I'm not the most naturally endowed woman, but I know how to stuff a bra. Well enough that a leech like Pete can't help but spiral into the honeypot.

But it's not for Pete.

Kane catches him staring and moves in closer. This is where the power game becomes confused. He wants to knock me down, but he also wants to protect his meat from other wolves. I call this the "douchebag's dilemma." He needs to defend without making me feel good about it. Y'know, so I don't get self-confidence or anything.

"You get that STD sorted out, mate?" Kane asks.

"Don't know what you're talking about."

Kane looks at me and feigns realisation. "Oh, right. Not in front of the lady. Sorry."

"Fuck off."

"It's only banter, Petey Pie. Lighten up."

Pete sinks back behind the bar and focusses on the drinks. I could almost feel their muscles flexing under their shirts, like two gorillas sizing each other up over a potential mate. This is why I laugh when people have trouble understanding evolution. The kind of person who gets offended when you say humans are animals, just like any other. In reality, we've barely branched off at all.

We take the drinks and move over to a spot by the window. I suppose I'm on display now. He's a fisherman showing off his catch. I can feel a couple of leers as strangers pass. It's dangerous—combining a short skirt with a high bar stool. I know that any attempt to force the fabric down a couple of inches will be entirely in vain.

"So, are you up for this?" he asks, knocking back half his drink. "Ain't nothing worse than flakers."

"Don't I look ready?"

He appraises me once more. I am a carcass in a butcher's window. I made sure of that. My dress is not only short, but tight as an adder's body wrapped around a fresh kill. It has a similar texture, too—an artificial scaliness as though it really is snake skin. It's a vibrant red to match not only my lipstick, but the sheen of my hair.

"You sure as fuck do."

"Then let's go."

"Finish your drink."

I know how to handle my liquor, but Kane doesn't know that. I skol my drink in one hit. Ironically, I think bartender Pete is on my side this time. Kane ordered a double, but this is a single shot at best. The vodka is weak as piss, overpowered by the tang of the cranberry juice. I suppose Kane's well known in these parts. And competitors don't like to help fellow predators.

I press my fingers to my lips, pretending to be flushed by the alcohol.

"Good?"

"A little strong," I lie.

A lecherous grin spreads across his face. "Don't worry, I have better shit at my place. Think of it as a practice round."

I wink. "Then let's get to the main event."

~*~

His apartment is just around the block, right in the heart of the clubbing district. I've heard about guys like this. They shit where they eat. Every night is a conquest, meeting up with a new Tinder hit, or perhaps a few. I'm sure he had a backup, in case I turned out to be either frigid or a dog.

On nights free of appointments, he'd go to one of his hunting spots. There, sipping water in the corner, he'd watch as women got drunk. Flocks of twenty-somethings celebrating a hen's night. Or university students enjoying Lady's Night a little bit too enthusiastically. Then, like a true hunter, he'd find the weak or isolated. He'd wait until they were separated from the pack, and then pounce. Maybe he'd move up to the last survivor, struggling to stay awake, and offer her a hit of cocaine to give them 'a second wind'. Or he'd console the crying bride-to-be, offering them one last night of fun at his place. *It's just around the corner. Nobody has to know.*

How do I know these things? Well, it's not my first rodeo. And before all this…well, I've been the victim. It happened once, but that was enough. Enough to change me. Enough to make me want to purge every last one of these motherfuckers from the world.

I've played other parts, too, but Tinder is my favourite tool, an easy way to rope in the douchebags. None of the setup and all of the reward.

"The bar is this way," he says. "Unless you want something stronger?"

Oh, Jesus. He really does have a bar in his house. It's in the lounge room, which looks like something out of an '80s interior design magazine. Think *American Psycho*. There are black leather lounges, adorned with a few stray silk pillows, which float atop the white tiled flooring like islands. Beside them is a small bar, made of what I'm assuming is faux black marble. The usual suspects sit behind it—Grey Goose Vodka, Glenfiddich, Blanton's. The real shit.

"How about Grey Goose and some coke?" he asks.

"Are you serious? Mixing that stuff is a tragedy."

He flops a baggy on the counter of the bar. The white powder is unmistakable against the black surface.

"Real coke," he says.

Ugh, I feel bad for getting dragged into his stupid joke. But then I convince myself it's for the best. I don't want him to think I'm too experienced. I want to look like a party girl, yes, but not yet jaded. I need that touch of naivety for him to exploit.

I look down, feigning embarrassment. "I don't know," I say, letting a hint of anxiety into my voice. "That stuff hits me pretty hard."

"C'mon," he says. "Trust me. This is good shit. None of that rubbish you probably scored before. Trust me."

"You swear it's good?"

"Pinkie promise."

He pours me vodka in a goddamn whiskey glass, at least three fingers high, and starts to prep the rack. Its gets a blast in the microwave, to dry it out, before he lines it up on the bar-top with a credit card. That explains the choice of black marble.

"Ladies first."

I take a sip of the Grey Goose. I won't lie, it's good shit. But I don't want to get tipsy. A little to calm my nerves is fine, but *fuck*…he's poured me enough to sedate a farm animal. And I don't know what else is in it. I've heard of men that pre-spike their drinks. You can see them pour it straight from the bottle, but you can never know what went into it beforehand. This may sound like paranoia, but why take the chance? I wait until he looks away, and spit my sip back into the glass. Yeah, I'm a class act.

"That's expensive stuff," he says. "Don't let it go to waste."

"Let me get a taste, first."

I pull a five-dollar note out of my bra. It's a garish pink thing with the Queen's smug face on it. I roll it up into a tight straw.

Kane scoffs. "You've gotta use better than that on this. I told you, this shit is legit."

He pulls out his wallet, black leather, and slides out one of many hundred dollar notes. I suppose he thinks money impresses a girl. I won't lie, I am a little aroused. Only because I know I'll be stealing it later. He rolls the note like an expert and passes it to me with a grin.

I hold out my hand. "You first."

"That would be rude."

"I don't know much about quality," I say. "I'd feel much better if you tested it before I do." I tug on the strap of my dress, biting my lip nervously. This exposes a little more of my cleavage. I see the fire burn in his eyes.

"Okay, but no pussying out. It's not fair to let a guy fly alone."

"Of course not."

He leans over the counter, positioning up the line.

Now, I may have a stuffed bra, but there's little else that can be hidden on my person. Like I said, my dress is virtually a second skin. But it doesn't take much to hurt a person. You'd be surprised what you can hide in a bra.

I reach into the plunging v-line of my dress and slip out a 'chicken fillet'—those silicone-like pads that are every ladies friend. Well, ladies from A to C, at least. There's a slit in the back, which I'd scored myself using a box-cutter. Inside it is a small metal rod, pointed on one end. It's no longer than two inches, and no thicker than a pencil. But it's enough.

Have you ever been bored on a bus? No doubt you've noticed the window-breakers, those little red hammers for use "in case of emergency." They can shatter glass with a single knock. This is a similar concept. Diamond tipped high-carbon steel. I clench my fist around it, letting the pointed end protrude slightly.

Sssnnnnnshh.

Kane snorts up the white powder.

Whoooosh.

I swing my arm through the air, using my shoulder for extra leverage. The point crashes down on the back of his skull.

C-Crack.

There're two noises, deceptively close together. They sound like a coconut breaking in two locations at once, milliseconds apart. What it really is are the joint sounds of my device coming down on his skull, and his face smashing against the marble bar. Okay, maybe it's not that different from a coconut after all. He collapses on the ground like a ragdoll. Powder drifts up into the air.

Extra pure, he said.

Well, that hit was extra clean.

I drag him away by his feet.

~*~

"Where's your collection?" I ask.

Kane struggles to look up at me, his head bobbing around like a buoy in the ocean. It was an even better strike that I thought—I can only imagine how fucked up his vision is right now, swirling double images, dancing like pink elephants. Why drug people when you can knock the shit out of them? Twice as fun and far less creepy.

"I said, where is your goddamn collection?"

"W-What collection?" he asks, the pieces in his mind congealing enough to form a picture.

"You know what I'm talking about."

"I do?"

Sigh. It seems what little intelligence he had has been smashed out of him.

"Guys like you," I say, "all have a collection. A trophy cabinet, so to speak. Polaroids of every chick you've fucked, tucked in a shoebox under the bed. Snippets of their hair. A drawer full of dirty panties. That sort of thing. Now, I don't know what your particular fetish is, but you're sure as shit going to tell me." I swirl my skull-knocking rod through my fingers, like a college student fiddling with a pencil mid-lecture. "Else, I send you back to la la land. *Tú entiendes?*"

"I don't have anything like that."

He struggles, realising just how fucked he is. His arms are duct-taped to one of his fancy leather chairs, wrapped over time and time again. No matter how large his 'glory muscles' are, there's no way he's working himself free. Should have spent a little time on your core, hey buddy?

"All right then," I say, stepping forward.

He tucks his head down. "N-No, wait!"

"For…?"

"You're a fucking psycho."

"And you're a predator. Your point?"

"You're not going to get away with this."

"I'm not? Oh, right. Because of the recording on your phone? I smashed that to bits. An iPhone? Really? Does everything in your life need to be douchey?"

He releases a low moan. This is my favourite bit—when they realise exactly how fucked they are. That I've done this before, and that I'll do it again. That they're just a little fly in one of my traps, wrapped up in web, struggling in vain.

"Okay, okay. I'll tell you."

"Hit me."

"The safety deposit box in my bedroom closet. The pin is 1-9-8-5."

~*~

I don't know what I expect to find when I swing open the door of his safe, but I like to think I'm prepared for anything. As I said, I've seen everything to the mundane to the super-creepy. This time, however, I have this twisted feeling in my gut, telling me to prepare for the worst. Maybe it's because of the size of the safe. I had expected the kind of safety deposit box you find in hotels, large enough for your passport and some cash, but nothing too crazy. This, however, is something out of a thriller movie. Half a metre in each dimension. The numbers beep as I punch them in.

"Show me what you got."

The door creaks open.

The smell hits me first. It's a pungent organic smell, sweet and sickly at the same time. Like rotting fish, sweat, and blood all mixed together in the bottom of a bucket. I dry-wretch, instantly regretting skolling that cranberry vodka. My stomach seizes but I deny it the pleasure.

I slide out a large folder. A folio, really—like something you'd display samples of your artwork in. It has metal rings down the spine, securing clear plastic sheets. I carry it to the bed and flop it down. It settles on the black silk sheets.

I throw back the cover.

Fuck.

The first sheet houses a piece of paper—a canvas, really. There are samples arranged in the loose shape of a girl. At the top, a clipping of hair, taped down to the page, some of the strands stained with blood. Clipping of photographs complete the face. A polaroid of each eye, Kane's fingers visible as they pinch back the eyelids. The lips are similar, but with visible cuts.

Beneath, there are five strips of skin. There's a little flesh still attached behind them, but they're otherwise pretty clean. They've been cut with a scalpel, stripped off with medical precision. A faint orange tint in the paper is the only evidence of blood, the fluids which have leached from the skin over time. They're arranged in the shape of a stick person. One long strip for the body, and smaller ones for each limb. At the end of each is a nail. Two are plastic–the kind of fake fingernails that women glue over their real ones–but the toenails are real. I can see the pieces of tissue that pulled away when they were pried off.

Oh, but that's not the worst bit.

I'm sorry.

Between the 'legs' is a cotton ball. I will let you guess where it has been shoved. Even through the plastic sheet, the smell haunts my nostrils. Blood and discharge and cum, all mingling together in a crusty, pale red pile.

My hands tremor. I flick through the catalogue. Each page is similar, only the details changing. The colour of the nails and hair. The degree of care taken with each cut. But by the end, I can taste blood in my mouth. This is by far the worst I've seen. And I thought I'd seen fucking everything.

"Kane?" I call out.

"Yeah?" comes the nervous reply.

"Where do you keep your tools?"

~*~

Kane screams while I work. That's to be expected. But his apartment is impressively sound-proofed. He really has thought of every angle. I learn to enjoy his protests, as he enjoyed those of his victims. His whimpers sound pathetic. It fills my heart with joy.

Now, I don't know exactly how he did it, but I like to keep my work true to life. So, I slice a strip of skin from each limb, placing them on the glass-topped coffee table in the shape of a man. The strip from his chest is my favourite. It encompasses part of his large chest tattoo, giving it a unique pattern. I make sure it's extra-large. It will be the centrepiece of my work.

"You're a sick bastard, aren't you?" I ask, as I slide the scalpel across his scalp.

To be fair to him, he only took clippings of his victim's hair. But, given that his hairstyle's rather short, I figure it's best to cut out a chunk of the whole thing— roots and all. The fierce look in his bloodshot eyes tells me that he doesn't appreciate my ingenuity. It remains while I extract each of the four nails. He really is a sour bastard. You think he'd appreciate somebody improving his art. Appropriation drives creativity.

"What am I missing?" I ask, looking at the specimens laid out on the table.

"Cotton balls are in the bathroom."

I smile broadly, slapping his cheek. "Oh, look at you! Helping me out now. My little man is growing up."

"Fuck you."

"Hmm, no. I'm afraid that part of the night has long bolted."

"You won't get away with it."

"Honey, I already have."

I walk to the kitchen. I can hear Kane struggling, grunts of pain as he once again tests the strength of his duct tape bindings. Idiot. You can't overpower duct tape. For somebody with a history of violence, he sure doesn't know shit about his craft. I slide a chef's knife from the block. It's Japanese, made of folded steel. I pause a moment, appreciating the pattern on the flats. Occasionally, tackiness and class intersect.

I return to Kane. The look on his face as I undo his boxer shorts is priceless. I really wish you could be there. His eyes bludge wider with every button that slips free. Not how you expected this to go, is it, prick? I laugh aloud at my own thoughts.

"Hmm."

"What?"

"Oh, nothing. It's not very big, is it?" I tap the back of the knife on my jaw, pondering the worm that lay shrivelled before me. "I guess I'm making a diorama. So, that's okay. I just didn't expect it to already be to scale."

"If I get out of here, I'm going to kill you."

"Please try."

I pull on his foreskin, stretching him out like fresh calamari, and press the blade against the base. He screams. A loud, piercing number. I wonder if his victims made the same cry? I doubt it. They would have been unconscious most of the time. I really am glad I never indulged in his bar.

"You know," I say. "From the moment I saw you, I knew I would swipe right."

I wink as I cut off his cock, swiping the knife across. Swipe right, indeed. I don't think he appreciates the joke.

My phone buzzes in my pocket. Kane's cries ring in my ear.

I slip it out, unlocking it with my thumb. There's a notification from Tinder.

I take a deep breath. Could I go two in one night? I still have a lot to do. Cleaning, for example. There's a mess of blood on my hands, and even more soaking into the couch. And I still haven't decided whether to kill him or not. Then again, it *is* Valentine's Day. A special day. Maybe I should treat myself?

Oh shit.

I've received a 'super like'. Allow me to explain: when somebody on Tinder *really* likes you, they can skip the 'swipe right' bit and choose to 'super like' you. That way, the object of their affection finds out about it regardless of whether they liked them back. It's the nuclear option. A little bit desperate, but you only get one per day.

Let's see.

David's smiling face greets me. Y'know, the perfect guy. Beaches and smiles and personality. Mr Pixar Film. I sigh.

I read his message.

<Hi, Mae. I know the super like thing is a bit desperate, but it's Valentine's Day, so I thought I would

take a chance. I haven't dated in a while, not since my Mum died of cancer. That's not a sympathy thing, but… sorry, I'm ruining this. I wanted to say that when I saw your profile, it triggered something inside my heart. I know there's a lot to you. I can see the depth in your eyes, the many layers that cover your heart, hiding your true self from the world. I know what it feels like. It's hard to move through life. It's even harder to fall in love. So, if you're alone tonight, like me… then I hope you'll consider taking a chance. I have wine, food in the oven, and for the first time in a long time…hope in my heart. All I want is your company. And your stories, if you'll share them. Happy Valentine's Day. David.>

I put down my phone. There are tears in my eyes.

"Happy Valentine's Day," I whisper.

I thrust the blade into Kane's neck. Blood spatters across my dress.

Keep the food warm, David.

Tonight, I'll take a chance.

~*~

94.2% (A Romance)
Nathan M. Beauchamp

~*~

A cascade of brown water sloshed over the edge of the toilet bowl, dousing the shag rug and Jonathan's slippers. His intracon implant released a healthy dose of downers, spreading through his veins like cold silver, calming him. He snatched up the plunger and set to work. But minutes later, his face flushed from plunging, the toilet remained filled with putrid water.

Jonathan stripped and climbed into the shower. It turned on automatically and adjusted to his preferred temperature. His intracon released more drugs as soapy water pooled around his ankles. The drugs dulled the sharp edge of his anxiety, but didn't fully alleviate it. He thought of linking to his wife, Letty. The stability of her unvaried emotions calmed him better than synthetic dopamine, but he didn't want to distract her at work. At least one of them had a job.

His landlord, Mr. Greggor, had insinuated that Jonathan and Letty were at fault for the backup. Jonathan swore they hadn't flushed rice, paper towels, bandages, cigarette butts, lima beans (*lima beans?*) or feminine hygiene products down the toilet. Of the last item, he was quite sure, considering Letty's particular hygiene requirements. After repeated denials of his landlord's accusations, Mr. Greggor eventually agreed to have a plumber come out and check the toilet.

His landlord arrived five minutes before the plumber. In that time, he made no less than three circuits through the apartment, opening drawers, poking into closets, and staring at the framed photographs atop the living room sideboard. He lifted the largest and peered at Jonathan and Letty's smiling faces with his small, close-spaced eyes.

"Nice dress," he said. "You really went all out."

"Letty wanted a traditional ceremony."

Mr. Greggor *harrumphed*, set down the photograph, and began leafing through a stack of magazines on the coffee table.

"I'd appreciate it if you'd stop touching our things," Jonathan said, voice empty of the indignation and authority he'd attempted to summon.

Mr. Greggor ignored him and paged through *Biosynthesis Today*. He smirked at the title article: *Human-Synthetic Relationships Increasingly Common*. "Common doesn't mean right," the landlord said, not hiding his scorn.

Jonathan's stress level skyrocketed. His intracon dosed him with more dopamine and began recording the conversation. If Mr. Greggor went too far, if he said something inappropriate…

Mr. Greggor tapped the asterisk-shaped scar on the left side of his shaved head that hid his own intracon. "Record away, boy, record away. Law says I can't discriminate about who I rent to. I know the law. But I don't have to like it."

The doorbell rang. Jonathan rushed to open the door. The plumber smiled up at him. "Drain backed up?"

He led her to the offending room, Mr. Greggor close behind.

She took a look at the toilet full of sludge and wrinkled her nose. "You have a clean out?"

"Clean out?" Jonathan repeated.

"In the basement," Mr. Greggor said.

The clean out proved to be a massive corroded pipe that ran from ceiling to floor. Rust powdered into the air when the plumber leveraged open the access with a huge wrench.

"How long has it been since you had the line to the street rodded out?"

"Hard to say," Mr. Greggor replied.

"Hmmm," said the plumber. She returned to her van and came back with a large plastic bucket. Inside, a length of scaled synthetic material wriggled like a python and raised a toothsome mouth. The plumber lifted it as a snake handler and fed it into the cleanout. It herked and jerked its way through the opening. Gurgling, scrapes, and bangs rang from within the pipe.

"Found something," said the plumber.

The rodding slipped backward, retreating from the pipe, its mouth full of what looked like dirty newspapers. It spat them into the bucket.

"Looks like napkins," said the plumber.

Mr. Greggor's frown became a scowl.

"Not ours," Jonathan said. "We use cloth napkins."

"We'll see," Mr. Greggor said.

The rodding made several more trips down the pipe, returning with a corroded copper spoon, wads of stringy roots, chunks of decaying yellow fabric and—

"Disgusting," Mr. Greggor said.

The plumber avoided eye contact with Jonathan. The rod slithered back down the hole, as if embarrassed by the large pile of condoms lying on the cement floor.

"It's in the lease," Mr. Greggor said. "Right there on page seventeen!"

"They're not ours," Jonathan said.

"You mean to tell me they're Gloria's? The woman's eighty-three years old!"

"Well they're not ours." *We don't use them*, he almost continued. Had never used them because Letty couldn't get pregnant. But there was more than one reason to wear a condom, like synth-borne STDs. And Letty was only 94.2% faithful. That left a 5.8% chance…

No. It wasn't true. Not again. Not Letty.

Upstairs, the apartment stank of shit. He flung himself down on the sofa, too numb to feel angry. Mr. Greggor had promised to tack the nine hundred-dollar plumbing bill onto the next month's rent. Since losing his job when the entire customer service department at Bruder's Clothiers was replaced with synth workers, money had been tight. Letty paid their bills working as an accountant in the city's finance department. She would be home in a few short hours. What would he say to her? What would she say to him?

He flushed the toilet several times and filled the bowl with bleach. He scrubbed every inch of the floor tile and grout. Sprayed air freshener. Opened the windows to let in the mild spring air. The whole while he imagined a line of men–human and synthetic–standing on the sidewalk outside the two-flat, waiting their turn. He saw again the pile of condoms–lemon, chartreuse, neon orange, pink, baby blue–a huge assortment in grotesque, carnival colors. His hands formed into fists. He thought of punching the wall or the mirror, but that would hurt and he didn't know anything for certain. Not yet.

Letty was 94.2% faithful. He'd paid extra for the highest possible faithfulness index. There had to be a logical explanation for the condoms. *Or,* he thought, *I've gotten very unlucky.*

After a string of failed relationships and broken dreams, he'd liquidated the inheritance he'd received from his grandmother and gone to buy a synthetic partner from PerfectMatch™. After reviewing the results of his pre-screening and psych profile, he sat down with Bell, the Relationship Coordinator, and looked at his potential matches. A friendly woman with storm-gray eyes and plucked eyebrows, Bell recommended a partner with strong traits in empathy, consistency, and faithfulness. A trio of holographic women rose from the crystalline surface of the desk. At one-eighth scale, they peered up at him with tiny, jewel-like eyes.

"Each of these will meet your needs," Bell said, "But I'd take a long look at Letty. She's a sweet girl."

The miniatures smiled, twirled, smiled.

Bell brushed them away, and the desk's surface became opaque again. Jonathan's intracon trilled, signaling receipt of the full prospectus on the three potential matches. He reviewed them—a light-skinned woman with a ski slope nose and green eyes; another with Hispanic features, short, dark haired, cute; and the last, a tea-and-cream skinned Middle-Eastern woman, wide-hipped, oval-faced, with a certain kindness to her eyes. Their names were Sarah, Brighton, and Letty.

Jonathan examined each, reading the subtle variations in their attribute scores, his eyes returning to Letty's profile again and again. "Why don't you offer partners with one-hundred-percent faithfulness?"

"We've found an inverse satisfaction curve when traits

exceed certain thresholds. It varies from trait to trait. Some, like dominance, for example, we cap in the mid-seventieth percentile. People tend to *think* they want more dominance than they actually do."

"But isn't that the point of the psych tests and screening? To get what we *need* versus what we *want?*"

"Certainly. But personal preference also plays a role in the selection process. No test is perfect. Which is why we offer a range for each trait. You will notice that we've tiered physical beauty, with potential matches below, at, and slightly above your own physical attractiveness as measured by the Bulwyer index. Most clients believe they'd be happier with a match far more physically attractive than they are. Testing reveals the opposite—increased jealousy and distrust are the most common results of such a pairing. While we can scale any of your matches up or down as you wish, we strongly recommend not straying too far in either direction."

Jonathan cycled through the three women once more. "I can understand why someone might not want a partner with an extreme level of dominance, or one not attractive enough or too attractive. But why would anyone want a partner that might cheat on them?"

"Almost without exception, they don't."

"Then why not give all your partners a hundred-percent faithfulness?"

"Because it doesn't work."

Jonathan's brows drew taut. "What do you mean it doesn't work? I thought you had full control over traits. That's what your commercials promise. 'Why trust random chance when you can use science to find your PerfectMatch?'"

"Oh, we can produce partners that are a hundred percent faithful. I meant that it doesn't work for you—

the consumer." Bell pushed back in her chair. "Would you like to see the real Letty? I can have her brought out. She's inactive, of course—we won't wake her until you've made up your mind, signed the release forms, and transferred your funds."

Jonathan *did* want to see Letty. Her dark brown eyes and curly, chestnut hair had quickened his pulse. But he also wanted an answer to his question. Bell was holding something back, and he intended to find out what.

"I'm the one paying the money," he said. "I want a partner I never have to worry about. Not even five percent of the time."

Bell tapped the surface of the desk with shiny, blue nails. "Listen, Jonathan. I understand where you're coming from. I really do. I know all about the failed marriage. The affair." He winced as she continued. "The chaotic string of relationships afterward. None lasted more than six months, I believe. But you have to trust me when I tell you that a guarantee of faithfulness won't make you happy."

"Well," Jonathan said, "since you know so much about me, why don't you tell me *why* it won't make me happy? Because never having to worry about my partner cheating sounds pretty damned good to me!" He realized he was standing, that his hands were trembling. He lowered himself back into his chair and rubbed the stubble on his face.

"Because you can't love someone that you control," Bell said in a hushed tone as she leaned over the desk, her eyes intent. "The reason PerfectMatch works is because we understand the psychology of desire. We tailor a partner that meets your psychological needs, that compliments you, that understands you. But they can't be *too* perfect, or people take them for granted. They become nothing more than another appliance. A personal assistant that sleeps with you. We're not in the market of selling organization or raw sexual gratification. Lots of other companies do both better than we do, but what we're selling is far more important."

The Relationship Coordinator reached across the desk and took his hand. "We're offering you a chance—and a very good one at that—for love. And love requires trust. If you knew someone could never leave you, if they had no choice in the matter, how could you love them? How could they love you?"

~*~

Jonathan snatched the wedding photo from the sideboard and stared at Letty's smiling face, white dress, soft curly hair falling beside the curve of her neck. He'd found her request for a wedding quaint, endearing. She'd insisted on a vintage ceremony, complete with vintage photographs rather than using recordings from guests' intracons. The photos had grown on him. He enjoyed seeing them each morning, but couldn't remember the last time he'd played the compilation of the recordings sent over by family and friends.

He sorted through his intracon, digging down through layers of social news, photographs, security keys, unread notes to himself, and Letty's daily messages that ran from mundane to kinky. He found the wedding recordings—dozens of point-of-views recorded by their guests' intracons—and linked them to the ceiling projector. The room filled with a chaos of images, fragments, a patchwork of perspectives and static images crystalizing into a "crowdie" or consensus rendering of the wedding.

The projector layered light over walls, the floor, his face. The wedding swirled around him. Here was the rental clergyman in his white-and-orange vestments; here his sister Cori in a green silk dress; here Letty, waving one of her lovely hands, the ring she had insisted he buy sparkling. Here he stands in the silly black tux and white bowtie, arm extended, taking her around the waist, sweeping her off her feet, lifting her for a kiss—

"Honey?"

He hadn't heard the door open. Letty walked through the margin of the imager and regarded her unchanged former self, her slightly-younger husband, the host of family and friends arrayed around them, soap bubbles rising into the sky, laughter, shouting, laughter.

"Honey?" she said again. "Are you okay?"

"Of course I'm okay."

"You don't look okay."

Jonathan stood and swept the crowdie away, leaving behind their plain, ordinary living room. "I just wanted to remind myself, is all."

"You don't like crowdies. They make you feel queasy."

"Do I look queasy to you?"

Letty tried to link with his intracon, to check his emotional state and vitals, but he blocked her. He stood with arms crossed, scowling. "You know what you said? At the wedding? Do you remember?"

"I said a lot of things. And you know I remember. I remember everything."

"Yeah, you sure as hell can," he said. "That's why you've got a job, and I don't. That's why I sit around here all day doing nothing. Makes me think the anti-synth demonstrators might have a point. Human work for the humans, right?"

"Oh honey, did you get another rejection? You'll find work, I know you will. You're so wonderful—"

"Shut the hell up," Jonathan said. Though no more than a whisper, Letty's head snapped back, her face whitening. Amazing, that affect. How real. How believable.

"What's wrong with you?" she asked. "You won't let me sync with your intracon. You're distressed, and you cursed at me. You've never cursed at me before. There was that time you cut your finger slicing an apple, but that was at the apple, not me. Why are you so angry?"

"The toilet overflowed today."

"It did?"

"Yes. A nine hundred-dollar bill tacked on to our next rent payment."

"What? That's not fair. It couldn't have been our fault."

"Not our fault, no. More like *your* fault."

"My fault?"

"Yes." He watched her, checking for signs of stress, for signs that she'd started to understand. But other than the confusion on her face, she looked much the same as she always did.

"I'm going out," he announced. "I don't know when I'll be back."

"Jonathan?" Panic in her voice, on her face.

He shoved past her, slammed the door. Stalking down the street in his slippers, cold without his jacket, Jonathan pulled up an image in his intracon and fired it to Letty. Colorful condoms lying in a wet pile on the cement floor. Then he powered it down and strode into the night.

~*~

Without his intracon, he couldn't order drinks at The Shuttlecock or buy a ticket to a show at the Cineplex. He'd already seen everything anyway. Since losing his job, he'd spent more and more time away from the apartment—watching movies, playing immersers at the gamer's den, wandering shopping centers featuring early-model synth mannequins with their strange, unseeing eyes.

He couldn't face any of that tonight. He wandered beneath blue-tinted streetlights as self-driving taxis circled the block, waiting for their next fare. The wind picked up and a saturating mist began to fall. His shirt clung to his chest. His feet went numb in his slippers. He was a fool. He should have thrown *her* out of the apartment, left *her* to wander the streets. He summoned the rage he'd felt after watching the crowdie, turning off his intracon before it could medicate him. He pictured Letty's wide-eyed confusion and seemingly genuine surprise and hurt. The liar! The faker! She was just like his ex-wife.

Yet that wasn't true. He hadn't purchased his ex-wife. Hadn't selected her based on an index of traits. He let out a humorless chuckle. *PerfectMatch*. The idea now appalled him. Synthetic or organic, all women were untrustworthy. Even those created in a lab.

His shivering became a compulsive tremble that set his teeth clacking. Rivulets of water ran down his cheeks and neck. He couldn't stay out much longer—he'd freeze to death. He should return, face Letty. Tell her how things were going to be.

Jonathan arrived back at the two-flat soaked, winded, but full of resolve. He found Letty sitting in the dark. Slumped over at the waist, she raised her head when he stepped inside. That round face, those loving eyes—for a moment he felt as though he was seeing her again for the first time. Ten-inches tall, smiling, turning on her axis, data points flashing in a cloud around her. *Dependability 87.7%. Wit 37.2%. Sexual Desire 58.5%*. Not a jokester, punctual to a fault, a desire for sex that matched his own.

"Why?" Letty asked, her voice ragged. "You shut down your intracon. You shut it down, and I couldn't reach you. You left me with that horrible picture…"

"I thought it would be different this time," Jonathan said. "I really did. The numbers looked great. Ninety-four point two percent faithfulness. I trusted you. I trusted you until today."

Letty took in a gasping, sucking breath. She tilted her head, pierced him with her no-longer-kind eyes. Lower lip bent into a quivering frown, she rose to her feet, rubbing her eyes with the sleeves of her wrap dress.

"You don't have a faithfulness index," she said. "You haven't been mapped out and charted, every aspect of yourself laid bare. You don't know what it's like to *know* yourself. Really, truly know." A calm came over her, a dispassion. "Let me show you something."

The ceiling projector filled the room with light. A familiar-looking woman walked toward them, red lips, black hair, wearing a low-cut, pink-pearl evening dress. "…and so, after weighing my options, I decided to go in for some synthwork," the woman said through a lustrous smile. "I'm so glad I did!" The voice also sounded familiar.

"Who is she?" Jonathan asked.

"Gloria," Letty said.

"Gloria who?"

"Our upstairs neighbor."

The woman in the commercial looked thirty-five or forty. Her skin glowed. She extended her hand toward the camera, beckoned, winked.

"Her synthwork turned out really well, didn't it?" Letty said. "Did you know she's going to appear on a reality show? *Synthed and Sexy.* Airs next month. Mature audiences only."

Letty launched a preview for the new show. A bedroom identical to theirs, right down to the ceiling fan and windows hidden behind yellowing vertical blinds. A naked woman on all fours in the center of the bed. A man kneeling behind her. Another man coming in from a hallway just like theirs, the one that led down the bathroom, a third man behind the second wearing a—

"Oh god," Jonathan said. "Turn it off."

"Looks raunchy, doesn't it?"

"Turn it off. Please. I don't need to see this."

The light disappeared, throwing the room back into shabby desolation, Letty a dim shadow in front of the sofa. "We're living beneath a celebrity."

"If that's what you want to call her."

"She's human," Letty said, as if that explained everything.

He'd known all along there had to be a logical explanation for the condoms. He'd always known it. His doubt was a temporary, fleeting thing. Now that he knew the truth, he would never doubt her again. Never. He reached for her, wanting to feel the warmth of her body against his, to breathe in her scent—

Her hand shot out, shoving him backward.

"Letty?"

"Turn on your intracon," she said.

"Letty, I'm sorry—"

"Turn it on!" The edge of her voice shocked him. He blinked, powered up the implant. An immediate dose of dopamine lapped at his consciousness. Letty's intracon requested connection—her internal voice connected to his, her feelings linked to his own. He closed his eyes and accepted.

The anguish that assaulted him overwhelmed his implant's ability to chemically rebalance his emotions. He saw a loop of time starting with him fleeing the apartment earlier that night. The photo of the condoms. Letty sitting alone on the sofa as she tried again and again to find him—frantic, terrified, alone. Her belief that *he* had sent the photo as an acknowledgment of an affair. To torture her. To break free from her.

He felt the full arc of her turmoil, culminating in a single realization, hard and sharp and unshakable in its finality. A realization formed from hidden, incomplete memories. A mosaic of terrifying moments, of arguments, of words spoken in anger. A crowdie of a different sort, assembled from rediscovered memories of their life together before her last reset back to default settings.

"I thought it would work this time," Jonathan said, voice dull.

"So did I," said Letty.

From outside came the sound of feet clumping up the stairs. Jonathan slumped to the floor. Letty opened the door to a team from PerfectMatch led by Bell.

"Jonathan?" she said. "Do you understand why we're here?"

He didn't reply. Letty leaned down, kissed the top of his head. "Goodbye, Jonathan," she said. "I'm sorry things turned out this way."

He sat on the floor as Letty descended the stairs. Bell offered him a digital pad. "You'll need to sign."

"You can't patch it over? Take her back to right after the wedding like you did the last time?"

The release form hung in front of him, blazing gold. Bell knelt beside him. "Three resets is the maximum. If we tried another, we'd risk destroying her. I warned you this might happen—that each reset made her more likely to remember the last one. I told you to be careful. With a ninety-four-point-two faithfulness index, it doesn't take much to create an irreparable breach of trust."

"Breach of trust? What does that even mean? I take

my medication. I have my intracon set to regulate my moods. I've done everything I'm supposed to, everything the psychologist advised. And Letty still managed to remember! That's not my fault, it's yours. It's Letty's. She's the one with the problem."

"She's exactly to specifications," Bell said.

"*Things* kept happening," Jonathan explained. "She kept giving me reasons to suspect her. Did you see the picture of the condoms? What was I supposed to think? What would any reasonable person have thought?"

Bell gave him a sad smile. "I don't know."

His intercom prompted him to connect to the form. Weary, eyes watering from the chemical soup pumping through his veins, Jonathan attached his signature.

"What will happen to her?" Jonathan asked.

Pausing at the door, Bell smiled down at him. "Don't worry about Letty. She'll be just fine."

Vision blurring at the edges, he watched the door close, sealing him away in the darkness of his apartment. Bell's words reverberated in his mind. *Don't worry about Letty.* He imagined Letty with a different partner, one capable of trusting her.

She'll be just fine.

Grief overcoming the warm fuzz in his head, fists pressed into his eyes hard enough to make him see purple spots, he knew the same couldn't be said of him.

~*~

After the End
Will Swardstrom

~*~

It'd been a long day. The easy pickings had run out long ago, and only the most dedicated survived. Food couldn't just be opened with a can opener anymore, and I was exhausted from a day spent trying to simply find enough food for a few more meals. A girl just couldn't catch a break these days.

The old farmhouse was creaky and might have been considered a renovation project even before 'The End'. From the dusty green shutters on each side of the windows to the tall grass growing up all around the large porch, the aging homestead was my home in every sense of the word.

I'd long ago chosen a house a couple miles outside a small town in Michigan. Well...what was Michigan. I used to love the city, but when everyone started dying, the constant death was just too much for me to take. Plus, all the creaking buildings surrounding me had flat-out spooked me every time I went for a walk. I needed someplace that didn't remind me of the time before. The only sounds out here were natural. The wind whipping through the trees on a spring day was the most noise I usually dealt with.

As I approached the house, I knew something was

different. Something was...off.

It had been years since I had seen another human. The face that disappeared from the upstairs window just now didn't even seem familiar.

For so long, I hadn't measured time in days or years. Just by how many wrinkles I could count in the cracked mirror in my bedroom. Now, someone was in that very bedroom. Human contact was valuable, but as I'd learned over and over, survival was Job #1.

As I walked up the now-dusty path, I looked for all my weapons; the machete in the mail box, the claw hammer under the porch, the rusted monkey wrench in the planter.

All gone.

My heart skipped about thirty-seven beats.

Whoever was in there had been scouting my position for a good while now. I slowly pulled my trusty pocket knife. It wasn't glamorous, but years of life on a razor's edge had taught me that glamour didn't count for squat when your death lurked behind each corner. I carefully palmed my blade, and opened the door. I expected a bare living room, cluttered with the primitive decorations left behind by the last home owner. Somewhere in the back of my mind, a voice screamed at me to leave. To haul ass and never look back. But something else was urging me on, pushing me towards whatever might be in my house. As soon as I opened the door, I knew I should have run.

"Hello, Sadie," he said. Luther. My husband. My DEAD husband. It was like I'd stepped back in time. He looked...alive. The smug asshole leaned against the doorframe on the far side of the room, as if he'd just finished making a cake in the kitchen. But there was no cake. The only smell I noticed was the acrid stench of the cigarette he held between his thumb and index finger.

I didn't trust myself to say a word.

"Surprised, huh?" He took a drag of his smoke. "I get it. You thought I was dead. Hell, I thought I was, too." He tossed the butt of his cigarette to the side, right at the edge of the floral-print couch that somehow pulled the room together. My eyes followed the path of the cigarette for an instant, but then I realized he was more dangerous than any fire. When I looked back at him, there was a devilish look in his eyes. He seemed to be laughing at some untold joke. "Get this, Sadie, the disease wasn't done with me, yet. It gave me a second life!"

I hadn't seen him for nearly seven years, but the last time I saw Luther, his skin was sloughing off. A victim of the virus. At least, that's what the doctors said. It was no less than the bastard had deserved after all he'd put me through. I had walked out of the hospital and never looked back.

"What do you mean?" I asked.

He straightened, stepping away from the door frame. I took a step back, and he paused again. "After you left me to die, I thought that was the end. It was, until those government scientists came around a few days later. The Luther you knew did die in that hospital."

"How…what do you mean?"

He grinned.

I hated that grin. Hoped I'd never see it again. Counted on it.

I was wrong.

"I'm the next evolution, babe. You and me, Sadie…we can change the world." He moved towards me again. I put out my free hand to keep him away.

"Don't touch…"

He pushed my hand out of the way and with a swimming motion, put his other arm out towards me. Years of life on my own had conditioned me. I instinctively sliced down his forearm with my blade. Blood raced down his arm. He didn't even scream. I watched in amazement as the flow of blood slowed to a trickle and stopped. Within seconds, the wound had sealed. It was as if I'd never pulled my knife out in the first place. The only evidence was a quickly drying red stain on the old wood floors.

I wasn't nervous anymore. I was flat-out scared.

"Oh baby, I wish you hadn't done that…"

Tales from the Canyons of the Damned

The Sparrows in Her Hair
Hester J. Rook

~*~

Red cheeked
the breeze tickles her back
soft as a careless whisper.
Her mouth is caramelised fig and salt tang
and she wears seaweed in her hair.
From the shore the waves roar, weaponised teal, flashing
bright
and the sky is purple haze
(as speckled as her nails, buried in the sand
fingertips deep in the cool moistness of the earth.)
She communes with the crabs, albino and soft shelled
as they scuttle into sand-tubes
and hide amongst the spinifex.
As the tide recedes she pries out pippis and splits them
sucking out juices with her scaled tongue
and hurling their smoked shells back into the sea.

And she waits.

The pregnant moon rises soft

and the world is still
for three heartbeats (one two)
(three). Then
her lover comes (ethereal as a spirit)
and the waters roil, waves gouging.
When her lover comes (dusk bathed, storm-woman)
the crabs flee deep into the dunes and
as finally
she steps silent from the sky onto sand
she licks the salt from the hollow of her throat
smiles through red lips
and kisses the sparrows in her hair.

~*~

James and the Gentry
Kevin Lauderdale

~*~

"Yes, oh, yes! Of course I'll marry you, Reggie! Kiss me!"

How on earth was I supposed to explain to Serena Wessox that not only had I *not* meant to ask her to marry me, but that I was, in fact, already engaged to Galia, First Princess of the Lande of Faerie?

Hang on! I'm not sure that's the place to begin with— Serena canoodling and my double jeopardy. Naturally, I remember Homer's *Iliad* from my days at school. Beginning *in media res* and all that. But I think I'd better, as those Hollywood chappies put it, rewind the reel. It began two days earlier.

Let's see…I was at home having a whisky and soda…Oh, yes, that's much better. Note to self: Whenever possible begin with a whisky and soda—a *large* whisky and soda.

I was relaxing at home in my zebra-striped armchair enjoying a rather large whisky and soda when James entered.

"Telegram, sir." My trusted valet proffered the yellow paper on a silver tray.

"It's from Flippy," I said after I had perused the missive.
"Sir?"
"Frederick Lidd-Jones. 'Flippy.' You remember the Lidd-

Jones estate, James. Huge pile down Hastings-way. The scene of last New Year's Eve's revels."

"Ahh, Liddston Hall. Of course, sir."

"I bet you remember. Didn't I see you chatting up that very pretty redhead of a lady's maid? Ummm…Molly, eh?"

"Miss Margaret is a devotee of the German metaphysicians, sir. We passed the time discussing Schopenhauer."

"I bet you did."

James cleared his throat. "I take it that we are leaving for Liddston Hall, sir?"

"Yes, indeed. ASAP. 'Come at once,' reads the epistle. 'Life or Death. Weather remains charming. Flippy.' Seven…eight…nine…that's Flippy for you. Ten words for a shilling and he's not going to waste a single one."

"I shall commence packing, sir."

I gave a nod of approval and set to work on the old W and S. It was a lengthy and arduous task, but I muddled through.

~*~

Is there anything more restorative to the soul than a picnic? To relax in the shade of a willow tree while your gentleman's gentleman unpacks salmon and watercress sandwiches from a hamper…to cool your feet in a babbling brook while sipping Chateau Peyraguey as your man peels your apple…to stroll about the verdant green of the countryside secure in the knowledge that all will be cleaned and packed away when you return from the old bucolic perambulations…

I heartily recommend it to one and all.

True, Flippy had said, "Come at once," but, even in this brave new world where mankind races about in two-seaters at the harrowing speed of thirty m.p.h., the niceties must still be observed. The sandwich is all that separates us from the animals. That and detachable collars.

While lunching, I had noticed a low fence not too far off in the distance. After handing my napkin to James, I set off to investigate in the hope that it might provide an amusing anecdote for use during dinner that evening. The fence was a typical country corral, about chest-high and made of rough-hewn wooden rails. A crudely lettered sign was nailed to it:

> Do NOT cross this
> Field unless You can
> Do it in 23 seconds.
> Our Bull can do it in 24.

Sure enough, there was a bull. You know the type: ring through nose, sharp horns, and about the size of my sofa.

I was appreciating him from humanity's side of the fence when I heard a soft cry of "Oh!" and then saw a flutter of pink at the opposite end of the corral. Something vaguely young-lady-sized and young-lady-shaped appeared to have fallen into the bull's domain.

This was a lady fair in trouble and that clearly came under the Rule of the Brubakers. And I, Reggie Brubaker, never shirk from the R of the B. Although I personally find women to be more trouble than they're worth, I feared the wrath of 32 generations of ancestors going all the way back to the Norman Conquest if I did not behave chivalrously.

I will draw the curtain of discretion over the ensuing 25 seconds. Suffice it to say, the bull acquitted himself in the best tradition of his breed, and later that evening James did yeoman's work cleaning my wingtips and repairing the seat of my pants with such tiny stitches that even my own tailor would not have known that they had gone adventuring.

The young lady and I soon both stood safely outside the bull's domain.

"Are you…" I panted, quite out of breath. "Are you hurt at all?"

She was about five feet tall and ten years younger than my three decades, and she seemed to glow with an inner light. Her hair, chic and short, could only be called "Titian" in color. Her eyes were the gray of the finest top hat ever seen at the Ascot races, and her ears slightly pointed at the tips. Her pink dress was gauzelike and unaccountably spotless. As I said, I've never really had much use for women, but this one was, in the words of the chaps down at my club, "A bit of all right." She was the very embodiment of glamorous.

"You saved me!" she said, throwing her arms around me.

"Um," I said, and then, as politely as one can in such circumstances, slowly extracted myself and took a step back. "Reginald Brubaker at your service."

"Oh, Reggie, I owe you my life, my everything…" she stepped forward, arms outstretched.

I took another step back and found my back up against the corral's rails.

She continued. "I will be yours forever and ever."

"Um, Miss . . ."

"I am Galia, First—"

"Miss First—"

"No, I—"

An "Ahem" came from my right. I turned to find James standing at my side, boar bristle clothes brush in hand.

James has that way about him, of being where he's needed at all times. Just when you think he's in the kitchen polishing up the long-spouted Georgian silver coffee pot, and you yourself decide that you'd like a gin fizz, suddenly there he *is*, bearing same. He just sort of manifests.

"Oh, thank you, James. The young lady . . ." I turned back to Galia, but she was gone.

I scanned the immediate vicinity. No Miss First. I stood on tiptoe to gain the advantage of higher ground. No Miss First.

Where she had stood there was now a small swarm—if swarm is the word I'm looking for—of butterflies. Little pink coves with red streaks. Quite nice. They hovered for a moment and then simply dispersed into the firmament (and I *know* firmament is the word I'm looking for).

"The young lady…" I croaked.

"Young lady, sir?"

Point to James. Not only was there no young lady, but there was nowhere to which a young lady could have dashed off.

James began delicately dusting my shoulders. "Perhaps your head, sir. I did not see a young lady, but I did see you make contact with the ground rather forcefully."

"Shook up the old bean, eh?"

"Quite possibly, sir."

I turned to my left. The bull was there sure enough and he almost looked like he was laughing. Prime rib was certain to be served for dinner at Flippy's, and I decided that I would have double helpings.

~*~

Flippy was not, as I had expected, waiting for me like a spaniel, tail and whiskers all aquiver with anticipation. I steered the two-seater up the gravel drive in front of the Hall (four stories of butter-colored stone accented with more leaded glass than, well, as the 16th century ditty runs: "Liddston Hall / More glass than bloody all") to find only the family majordomo, Cliveson, in attendance.

"Welcome, Mr. Brubaker." He turned and exchanged barely perceptible nods with James.

"Flippy about?" I asked.

"Mr. Lidd-Jones is down by the folly, sir."

Just as anyone can go from "crazy" to "eccentric" by the infusion of enough ready cash, an eyesore may be elevated to "folly" if the estate it adorns is large enough.

I sighed. My *raison d'être* for biffing down from London was that this was a supposedly urgent matter. To learn that Flippy was at that marble construction built by the fourth Baron Liddston with the dome of a mini-Parthenon and the columns of a mini-Acropolis when he should be here filling me in on the *r.d.* did not warm the Brubaker heart.

Nonetheless, I set off across the manicured lawns. The Rule of the Brubakers requires that I never turn down a friend in need. This I repeated to myself as I strode over the hill and down into the valley (both also constructs of the fourth Baron) and soon arrived at the folly.

There were two figures leaning against the columns and talking.

"What ho!" cried one of them, waving to me. Flippy.

The other I could not quite make out in the shadows cast

by the dome until—

"Hawr! Hawr! It's Reggie!"

Serena Wessox! The very byword of the horsey set for two seasons now. A girl whose slaps on the back had dislocated more than one shoulder. Not that she was particularly large, but she was *solid*. And, while her splendid profile was admired by all who saw it, her cries of "Tally Ho!" at the start of a fox hunt were known to temporarily deafen her party and her hounds. I simply found her to be...too much.

That we had been briefly engaged a while back I will chalk up to misplaced youthful exuberance. She had called it off after I had expressed reluctance to wear the traditional "hunting pink" coat while foxing.

"Reggie!" she exploded. "Flippy said you'd be stopping by." She let me have one of the best on my back and I lurched forward a yard. "What brings you down? A spot of fishing? I know a capital pool. Brought home three brown trout only last week. One was a ten-pounder!"

"Flippy called me down," I wheezed.

"Did you, dearest?" she asked Flippy.

Dearest? This was an innovation.

I said, "Yes. Said it was a matter of life or death."

"Really, sweetness?"

Sweetness? I was beginning to detect a trend.

"Um." Flippy stepped back and was jerking his head in the direction of Serena. "Um."

"Had it something to do with your neck?" I asked. "Seems to be all right now."

Before he could reply, Serena put both hands on my shoulders, spun me round to face her, and said, "Been a long time. Been a dashed long time."

"Oh, surely not that long."

"Long enough." She looked me up and down. "Well, Reggie..."

"Yes," I said.

She looked at me more intently. "Well, well, Reggie."

"Yes, yes, indeed," I replied.

"Well, well, *well*, Reggie." Now she smiled broadly at me.

"Yes, um. Indeed."

Her eyes took on a certain sparkle. I knew that look. Her eyes had sparkled like that in the early days of our engagement.

Another flicker of light caught the corner of my eye.

"What's that on your hand?" I asked.

Her left hand shot behind her back. "Oh," she looked away and then back at me with resignation. "Flippy and I are . . . engaged." She slowly dragged out the hand in question and I saw that it was adorned by a very respectable solitaire accented with emeralds.

"Are you? Oh, good show!" I breathed the proverbial inner sigh of relief. The Brubaker charm being not inconsiderable, those looks of hers were beginning to make me wonder exactly who exactly "Dearest" and "Sweetness" were. But no. My presence was not rekindling what the poets call The Flame of Love. An engagement ring was a sealed deal. Flippy was D and S and that was all there was to it. I need not ask for whom the eyes sparkled; they sparkled for Flippy.

"Ah," I said, turning to Flippy. "That must be why you wired me. To come on down and hear the good news in person."

Flippy was standing just behind Serena and shook his head rapidly. When she turned to face him, his head froze and his visage took the grin of a lad who, when caught with his hand in the biscuit tin, is about to pretend that he was actually putting something in.

But what he said was, "Oh, yes, of course. Engagement. What else? Now I really must dash. Must see Cliveson about . . ." Whatever he meant to say was lost to the ages as he took off like a roman candle towards the Hall.

Serena said, "Well, I've simply got to go down to the boat house and . . . uh. Say, Reggie, I don't suppose you'd like to . . . come with me?"

"No, I'd better go see what room Cliveson has given me. Last time it was too far from the kitchen. James complained mightily. Something about hot water bottles and the cooling effect of travel time."

She touched the lapel of my tweed coat with what can only be called a lingering caress. "We're dressing for dinner. See you then." She winked and trotted off.

~*~

I had trudged about halfway back to the Hall when out of nowhere—

"Strawberries, Reggie?"

Now, as I said, James has a habit of just sort of suddenly being there. While I hadn't exactly grown used to it, it no longer startled me.

But I was nearly knocked nadir over apex by the instantaneous arrival of Galia First bearing an ebony bowl full of strawberries. Huge, luscious examples they were, some nearly as big as a fist.

"Strawberries?" she entreated.

I took a bite of one. It was de-lish and I said so.

"Anything," she said, "to please my fiancé."

"Fiancé?"

She nodded enthusiastically and smiled beatifically up at me.

I said, "You appear to be laboring under a misapprehension, Miss First."

"My name is Galia, First Princess of the Lande of Faerie. And you, Reggie, are my betrothed. We shall wed upon the next full moon . . . um, a week Tuesday."

"When exactly did this engagement take place?" I certainly had no recollection of it.

"You saved my life. Of course we're engaged."

I had stopped walking after the first use of the word fiancé. The sun was just setting and its rays shooting out behind Galia gave her a shimmering halo. She was lovely, and for half a moment I was tempted. But, although I am descended from a long line of Brubakers who did marry, I had long ago put the notion behind me. I much prefer my carefree bachelor life: bopping down to Monte Carlo on a moment's notice, no one to tell me what not to eat or drink.

"But," I said, "I'm so much older than you. Surely you wouldn't want—"

She lifted her nose in the air. "I am one hundred and twelve. I am of age and old enough to know my own mind on such matters." Galia surveyed the acreage. "What a funny little place," she said. "Is this yours?"

"I—"

"You know, Reggie, it took me a long time to find you. You have a very difficult ethereal essence to follow. I've been looking for you all afternoon."

Over the hill came a tall, slim figure bearing a tray.

"Ah, James," I said.

"James?" Galia asked.

"My valet. I'm sure he'll be able to straighten this out."

She gave a superior sniff and then twisted, like a Christmas cracker's wrapping, off into nothingness.

James and his tray proved to be bearing a gin and tonic.

"Did you see that, James?"

"Yes, sir."

"What do you make of it?"

"Magic, sir."

"Not a trick of the light? Mirage?"

"No, sir. That was, I venture to assume, the young lady of whom you spoke after your luncheon adventure?"

"Yes."

"Most intriguing."

"Serena's here too."

"Miss Wessox?"

"Yes. James?"

"Yes, sir?"

"I may be engaged, but I'm certainly not getting married."

"Indeed, sir."

~*~

After a very good meal (prime rib, as presaged; Serena in a gown positively bedecked with décolletage) and the port having been passed, Flippy and I repaired to the billiards room. I called in James. Whenever a situation grows sticky, I always take it to James. You can trust his melon to steer you through the fog.

"Now, Flippy," I said. "We need to batten down a few facts. Item: you are engaged to Serena."

"Yes."

"Query: why did you call me down here?"

"I don't want to be engaged to Serena."

I nodded sagely. It was yet another example of the eternal triangle that would confound even Pythagoras himself: man, woman, and R. Brubaker, called in to set things right.

"That's very fine for you," I said. "Or rather, not so very fine. But, in the course of coming to your aid, I seem to have become engaged myself." I described The Mysterious Affair of the Bull Pen and the Strawberries and ended with, "James believes that the mystical is involved."

Flippy walked to the sideboard and poured himself a large one. "Were her ears pointed?" he asked.

"Now that you mention it, yes, slightly."

"The Gentry," he muttered. "Of course it's magic, Reggie. The ears. How could you not see she was a faerie?"

"But I know so little of fashion. I simply assumed that's how girls were wearing them this season."

"'Wearing' their ears…?"

I shrugged. "I quite agree. I don't understand the rage for those bell-shaped hats either." I turned to James for validation and he nodded in agreement. "But by faerie, do you mean like leprechauns? The little people? That spotlight effect in that play? 'Clap your hands if you believe—'" "That's the stuff of the past, Reggie. Everyone 'round these parts knows about the *real* . . . well, we call them 'the Fair Folk', or just 'the Gentry'. And they're not little. They're as big as any of us. They look more or less like us except that the women are always beautiful and the men handsome. They show up every generation or so."

He knocked back his drink, then poured another and continued.

"They always cause some kind of trouble. They're the

reason my Aunt Matilda's hair is dark. She was born blonde, you know. But a pair of the Gentry turned up at her wedding back before The War, and the lady of the two said she thought Matilda would look better as a brunette. Suddenly she was. And no amount of peroxide or anything else has been able to restore it." He took another sip. "Now it looks as if they are venturing out again. Or at least one is."

"So, we're both in the soup without a paddle. Dash it, there must be a million ways to get unengaged to a girl."

"Name one."

"Well, there's…Yes, you're right. It's impossible." I turned to James. "Two engagements to be ended. What do you say, James? Grab the old grey matter and give it a squeeze."

"With Mr. Lidd-Jones's permission, I will address your predicament first, sir. It is the more complex."

Flippy nodded.

"Beginning with first principles," began James, "if you save a faerie's life, it is then indebted to you."

"Ah," I said, "so all I have to do is make it clear I'd rather have a pot of gold instead of her hand. That should square the deal. Oh, wait, faerie gold isn't worth anything. It turns to dew on the morn or some such."

"So we are told, sir. But I do not think that the young . . . *person* to whom you are affianced possesses any gold. In the case of faerie princesses, they have only one gift to bestow: themselves. Any mortal man saving a princess is rewarded with a betrothal."

"Why would anyone want that?"

"It is my understanding, sir, that Princesses of Fairie are unparalleled in loveliness and all that any man might desire."

"Well, I don't desire Galia."

"You, sir, are not just any man."

I nodded emphatically. We Brubakers are made of sterner stuff.

"But why," I asked, "would *they* want us? I mean, a betrothal is a beast with *two* backs and all that."

Flippy said, "Yes, I've never understood why a lady of the

Gentry would want–no offense, Reggie–*you*, or for that matter any village blacksmith who just happened to save her from a bull when she could have a Prince of Fairie."

"The Gentry," said James, "are immortal. We are not."

"Ah," I said. "Even a blacksmith with muscles as strong as iron bands must eventually age and perish."

"Or be killed off," said Flippy. "I think I get it. We're toys to them. They grab one of us, have a few decades of fun, and then move on to another."

"Rather like keeping goldfish, eh?" I said.

"A trenchant simile, sir," said James. "History is rife with men in entanglements such as yours."

"And how did they get out of it?"

Jeeves arched an eyebrow.

"Or didn't they?" I asked, the proverbial sinking feeling gathering in my tum.

"They are simply never heard from again, sir. They go off with their princess to the Land of Fairie and…"

"And what, James? What, what?"

"Nothing, sir."

"Well, I'm not going to have nothing. I'll just have to break the engagement, that's all. It goes against the Rule of the Brubakers, but better a Brubaker with no Rule than a Rule with no Brubaker. Though I don't relish the thought of hurting Galia's feelings." I looked over in the mirror across the room. Poor girl. She never really had a chance. A devastating face like mine doesn't grow on trees. And it is not unknown for members of the fair sex to turn my way while I am strolling the Strand in order to get a second look. Especially when I am wearing my periwinkle tie.

"That might not be advisable, sir."

"Why not?"

"History does not recount any instance of a–you will excuse the use of the phrase, sir–mere mortal successfully breaking with one of the Gentry. Their anger at being rejected is, I understand, legendary."

"'A woman scorned' sort thing, eh?"

"To the utmost degree, sir."

"Possible lawsuit for breach of promise and all that?"

"More likely being torn to pieces by golden stags, sir."

I swallowed hard. I'd once been nipped in the ankle by my Aunt Gladys's Pekingese. The pain had kept me in bed for a week. This, I imagined, would be much worse.

"If, however—" James began.

"Yes, yes!" I was champing at the bit like any blue-ribbon bit-champer you care to name.

"If *she* were to break the engagement, sir—"

"Yes, yes! Then what?"

"That might make your position more tenable, sir."

"Ahhh. Good old James. Knew you wouldn't let me down. How do we go about arranging that?"

"I do not know, sir."

Enter the sinking feeling for an encore.

Flippy said, "All of this is very fascinating, Reggie, but it doesn't go anywhere near solving *my* problem. I'm engaged to Serena. And I need to . . . disengage."

"You could try my method," I suggested.

"Serena already told me about that. Too late. I've already been foxing with her twice. In full dress hunting pink."

"Indeed," said James as he turned his head in thought. It is upon such turns that my world continues to spin.

"Yes, James," I said. "Have you a thought? An inspiration? Is the spark of the divine about to leap from your lips?"

"I believe so, sir."

The sun rose again in my heart, spreading rosy-fingered dawn to all the bluebirds.

"Good old James!" I said. "Never doubted you for a nonce. Let's have it."

"I believe that we should seek out the feminine view pertaining to this matter."

I was nonplussed, but Flippy saw the angle at once.

"Of course!" he said. "*We* don't know how to break up with a gal, but *another gal* would. A stroke of genius, James. Reggie asks Serena how best to break it off. Pose it as a hypoth- . . . um, hypno- . . . um, 'Merely-A-Question' sort of question. Then we do it."

"You mean," I asked, "that if Serena says that no young lady would stay engaged to a chap who wears a check-patterned waistcoat with evening dress, we dash out and both buy half a dozen of the things to wear at every meal?"

"Precisely, sir," said James.

"Do you really think that whatever shocks La Wessox would apply to a Princess as well?"

"All the more so, sir. A member of the Gentry would have even more refined sensibilities."

I nodded. "Very well then. Tomorrow morning I'll speak with her. I shall be discrete."

~*~

I found Serena strolling through the rose garden. It was one of those plots of land populated by several species of the ol' red, reds and surrounded by a waist-high hedge.

"Hello, Reggie," she said, putting both hands behind her and leaning in towards me.

"Ah, morning, Serena. Look, I've got something to ask you."

"Oh, really?" The sun must have been in her eyes because she batted them fiercely.

"Yes. Dashed important," I said. "Before it's too late and all that."

"Yes, Reggie." She kept her lips slightly parted in a most disconcerting way.

"There are times when a chap has to say certain things to a girl—"

"Yes, Reggie." She was swaying back and forth very lightly.

"And it can be difficult to know exactly how to ask—"

"Yes, Reggie." She had a look in her eyes—a faraway look that led me to wonder if she was even listening to anything I was saying. Still, replace the word "Reggie" with "sir" and it could have been a conversation with James. And he always catches the drift. I trudged onwards.

"Um, Serena, now. Could you—or, rather, *would* you—?"

She stepped forward.

"Yes, oh, yes! Of course I'll marry you, Reggie! Kiss me!"

How on earth was I supposed to explain to Serena Wessox that not only had I *not* meant to ask her to marry me, but that I was, in fact, already engaged to Galia, First Princess of the Lande of Faerie?

How indeed?

I pushed her away, jumped over the hedge, and ran.

~*~

Half an hour later, after taking what I hoped was a Wessox-proof, circuitous route back to the Hall, I charged down to James's quarters.

I was just about to knock on the door when I heard from the other side a female voice say, "Oh, come on now. You can't possibly know it's him." The door opened and Molly the lady's maid stood there, her eyes suddenly widening so much that I thought their whites would reach to her mop cap.

"Oh, beggin' you pardon, sir" she said, her face blushing deep crimson. She curtsied and ran off down the hall.

I stepped in. There were two glasses and a bottle of Madeira on the table.

"Did it go well, sir?"

"I—"

The door flung open behind me and in charged Flippy, who nearly ran me over. "I've just had the most remarkable conversation with Serena. She's broken our engagement. And it didn't even require me dropping a few guineas on a waistcoat. Checkered or not. How ever did you accomplish it, Reggie?"

"It's all very simple," I said, "Now Serena wants to marry *me*!"

Flippy positively beamed. "Well, that solves my problem." He turned to James. "Your plan worked like a dream. Good job, old man!"

"That wasn't his plan!" I turned to James. "Was it?"

"Not per se, sir. However, this outcome was part of a back-up strategy of mine related to your mutual predicaments."

I stood there, my mouth agape. "Meaning?" I managed to stammer.

"Recalling your previous entanglement with Miss Wessox, a shift of affections was a possibility."

"But there are still two engagements to be broken. Only now they're both to me."

Flippy said, "But don't you see, Reggie, James has simplified the battle. Now there's only one front to fight on instead of two."

"I don't care if this is exactly the sort of tactic Napoleon would have used, it hasn't helped me."

James said, "If you will simply take two of your visiting cards, sir, and write on the back of both of them, 'Meet me in the rose garden at four p.m.,' I believe that will be sufficient."

"Sufficient for what?"

"To solve your dilemma," said James. "Leave everything to me."

~*~

James, Flippy, and I crouched behind the south end of the rose garden, well-obscured by bushes in bloom. Serena had arrived five minutes early and was pacing. We three watched James's pocket watch as the seconds ticked away until at exactly four o'clock.

"Who are you?" asked Serena.

We looked up and through some that which by any other name would smell as sweet to find that Galia had arrived.

"I'm Reggie's fiancée," said Galia. "Have you seen him? He was to meet me here."

"But *I'm* Reggie's fiancée," said Serena. "He was to meet— He's already engaged?"

"He's already engaged?"

"Why, that rat! It's off!"

"That weasel! It's off!"

"That ferret!"

"That...Ooooo!" Galia's face turned positively vermillion with rage. "That scoundrel! That charlatan! I'll have him torn to shreds!" She fell to her knees in rage. "I'll call upon Herne the Hunter to loose the stags of—"

"No, no, my dear," said Serena, reaching out and patting Galia's shoulder. "It really isn't Reggie's fault."

"It isn't?"

"No. He's weak, you know. All men are. He really can't be held accountable for the way nature made him: flighty and capricious."

"But he deceived us both." Galia stood up and thrust her fists into the air. "We must wreck vengeance upon him!"

"Sweet Reggie? No, no my dear…Some day he will marry, and then he'll settle down. Until then, he is to be pitied."

"He is?"

"Oh, my dear, you are still innocent and romantic, aren't you?" Taking Galia's arm, Serena led her towards the folly. "When you've been around as long as I have…"

They set off chatting quite companionably. Only when they had disappeared over the hill did I exhale and turn to James.

"*That* was your plan? To get them to hate me?"

"And thus to exercise a woman's prerogative to change her mind. Yes, sir."

"But Galia was about to exercise it by turning me into a pincushion for golden stag horns!"

"There is always a calculated risk with any plan, sir."

Flippy said, "James, I know Molly took the note to Serena, but how did Galia get hers?"

"Also Miss Margaret, sir. Her family has lived in these parts for ten generations. As such, they have a certain affinity for the land and its mysteries."

"Good grief," I said. "She's not a . . . Gentry, is she?"

"No, sir. But she has an aunt who is the seventh daughter of seventh daughter. I believe she keeps a finch which can travel to and from the Lande."

Flippy said, "I suppose you two better hot-foot it out of here. Despite this happy ending, Reggie's going to be *persona non grata* in these parts for some time."

I looked at James.

"The two-seater is already packed, sir."

"Will you be all right, Flippy?" I asked.

"Oh, of course, Reggie. Remember, Serena broke it off with me—and for one of my best friends! No, she'll be off on the next train, you can be sure. And I know better than to save any girl I meet with pointed ears."

"Cheerio, then."

"Cheerio."

We parted and I asked James, "What was that ditty about the fellow who gets engaged, but then never actually has to marry the gal?"

"Perhaps you are thinking of 'Evangeline,' by Henry Wadsworth Longfellow, sir."

"That's the one. Great stuff. 'This is the forest primeval' and all that."

"If you will recall, sir, the prospective bridegroom, one Gabriel, son of the blacksmith, is parted forcefully from his affianced before their nuptials and does not see her again until many decades later, just before he dies of a pestilence."

"Ah, but dies unmarried."

"If that was any consolation to him, sir, the poet did not record it."

"Still, James, there's no denying that it's a course of action worth examining."

"As you say, sir."

~*~

Hells Zoo:
Valentines Day Exhibit
Jessica West

~*~

"I'm so sorry Adriana. We should have stayed together.
Welcome to Hell Zoo.

My name is Tiba Bato, and I'll be your guide for Hell Zoo's special Valentine's Day Exhibit.

Take a good look at your surroundings. Before we proceed, you'll need a basic understanding of the layout of the exhibits and each enclosure within. I won't go over this again, so pay attention now.

Behind me is the entrance to one of our exhibits. Look at the path before you. A wide, white stripe is painted on either side of the dark asphalt path to offer high contrast and good visibility even in dim lighting. Within the enclosures, black lights in the ceiling make those lines stand out even more.

Do not touch those white lines. Walk single file along the neon green line in the center of the path. The path itself is broad enough so that even if you trip, you should not come close to the lines on either side as long as you follow the center stripe. Remember, this is for your safety.

Between each habitat is an oasis like the one we're standing in, with bottled water and clean restrooms. We will take a ten-minute break between each habitat. Because of how the stories are impressed upon your minds, the long breaks are required.

There's no need to raise your hand, Mr.?

Spaulding. Thank you. Ah, exactly how are the stories 'impressed?'

You didn't read the brochure, did you? Well, in that case, I'm glad you asked now. How many of you neglected to read the brochure? A show of hands, please.

Only three? Good. All right, then. Put simply, I am a nightmare demon. Not evil, Mr. Spaulding, I assure you. I am what's called a Trustee. I'm from the Purgatory exhibit. As it pertains to the tour, I act as a conduit from the mind of the sinners, monsters, or demons within each habitat to the minds of our guests. I offer you a glimpse directly into their memories and allow you to relive them almost as though they were your own.

My powers are strictly limited to this function by the wards below, above, and around us. You are quite safe with me.

Uh, I'd rather not...

Of course, I understand, Mr. Spaulding. One of our human guides will see you out.

Liam, please escort Mr. Spaulding–and anyone else who didn't read the brochure and would like to leave at this point–to the exit.

For the rest of you, Liam, Oliva, and Noah are human. As long as you remain between the white lines, you're safe.

Now, if you're ready to proceed?

Oh! Mr. Spaulding. Decided to stay, did we?

Well...there are guards here. Three of them and only one of you, so...

We prefer the term *guide*, but if it makes you feel better to think of them as guards, then, by all means, do.

Now, before we begin our tour, please listen carefully and keep the following rules in mind.

1.) For those of you taking the regular tour, at the entrance of Siren's Island, you'll be given a pair of earphones. Use them. Each pair comes in its own package and they are disposable, so I can assure you they are sterile. No one has worn them before you. If you are unable to wear them, for whatever reason, you'll be escorted around the island to wait for the rest of the group.

2.) No food or drinks of any kind are allowed in the enclosures, especially salt and fluids. Salt is used in many wards and sigils. It's how we're able to keep our guests out of harm's way while still allowing them full view of the enclosure they're passing through without any visible barriers to obscure the sinners, monsters, or demons from view.

3.) Remain, at all times, on the path. The undersides of the paths themselves are also warded, and this is for your protection. While your guides are capable of subduing stray sinners, demons, or monsters until a keeper can recast the sigils, they will not be able to protect you in the meantime.

4.) If you have any sort of supernatural nature, even to a small degree, you should not enter Hell Zoo's enclosures under any circumstances. While the wards are designed to keep the demons, sinners, and monsters inside their habitats, they were not designed with psychics, telekinetics, or other innocuously imbued humans in mind. We have no idea how our wards will affect the gifted. Before we proceed, you will be asked to sign a waiver. We cannot be held responsible for anything that might happen to you as a result of the wards.

Now that we've gotten that out of the way, read over your waivers and, if you're certain you have no supernatural abilities whatsoever, go ahead and sign them.

When you're ready, you may choose which exhibit you'd like to enter. There's the standard tour that's open year-round, and the special Valentine's Day exhibit you see behind me. Those of you who wish to take the regular tour, please follow Lili here. The rest of you, follow me.

~*~

Richard Bishop stepped out of the cab, taking care to remain under the umbrella's circumference, though it offered little protection from the

torrential downpour. Within seconds, he was safely encased in the foyer.
But in those seconds, his pants legs managed to get soaked.

"My apologies, Mr. Bishop. Shall I get you a towel?"

"No worries, Jefferey. You can hardly help the weather, now can you?"

The attendant chuckled.

Richard continued toward the elevator before the man could pursue a conversation. The attendant was polite and, indeed, attentive, but he had better things to do tonight.

"Have a good evening, Mr. Bishop."

He pressed the button to call the lift to the ground floor. "You as well, Jefferey."

He was cordial but brief. The attendant would understand. Although Richard didn't care one whit about him, he did have an image to uphold; one of kindness, compassion, and generosity. And he truly was those things, but no one could be expected to be so inherently *good* all the time. Today, he didn't have time to be overly generous, to stay and chat with Jefferey. Mary would arrive within the hour, and he needed to be ready.

Tonight was the night. As he rode the elevator to his apartment on the eleventh floor, he relived the last three months. An exceptional seduction took a bit of time and patience, but he felt the thrill of the chase no less than if it had occurred in seconds.

The first time he saw her, Mary was leaning over a rack of vegetables at the market, her large breasts barely contained by a department store bra. He circled around and returned, this time in the same isle. The view from behind was just as good; but to know for sure if she was the one—the next one—he had to see her face.

Sidling up beside her, he lifted a cucumber and pretended to examine it carefully. Glancing at her, then back at the cucumber, he cleared his throat.

"Excuse me, miss? Could you tell me...Well, I'm afraid I don't know how to choose a good vegetable?"

"Oh, sure." She glanced at him, then immediately looked away.

Shy. That was good.

"I mean, I'm no expert…"

Timid, too. Very good.

"Um, I usually squeeze them." A deep blush spread across her cheeks.

So, innuendos weren't lost on her. Even better. Not completely oblivious but easy to control. Mary was exactly what he was looking for. And now, after three months of softly wooing her, she was his.

He was so proud of how far she had come in so little time. She would make some lucky man very happy one day.

The elevator chimed and the doors opened onto his floor. Only by strength of will was Richard able to keep himself from running to his apartment.

His hand trembled with excitement as he opened the door. Richard stood in his foyer, letting the door swing shut behind him, and looked at the pristine beauty he'd surrounded himself with over the years.

He inhaled deeply through his nose, gaining strength from the neat, clean atmosphere around him and the subtle scent of freshly laundered linens and chamomile. Pushing the breath out through his mouth, he expelled the last of his anxiety and thought of Mary's plump lips.

She would come to him bearing all the gifts he'd bestowed upon her over the last few months. His favorite, though, would be the grape lip gloss he'd given her last week. It may have been a cheap gift, especially compared with others he'd given her, but he couldn't wait to taste it on her lips after…

Richard nearly came apart right there in the entry, thinking about what lay ahead. He quickly made his way toward the master bedroom, and headed straight for the shower. Once there, he used the shower gel Mary had responded to the best. Never let it be said that Richard didn't study his ladies carefully. He knew exactly what she preferred, and tonight had to be perfect.

When he finished bathing, he took himself in hand and worked up a fresh lather with special soap. Made from natural ingredients, this soap was gentler on the more sensitive flesh. Slippery and warm, he stroked and squeezed. Rather than prolonging his pleasure, as usual, he made quick work of it. This wasn't an exploration or indulgence in fantasy. This was prep work.

With thoughts of the night ahead in his mind–a vision of Mary's glistening lips around him instead of his hand–Richard let loose with a shuddering release.

He dried off and dressed as quickly as possible, the languid relaxation he usually experienced after orgasm held at bay by his excitement.

With his bathrobe wrapped around him, Richard made his way into the library to fix a drink and wait for Mary.

He didn't have to wait long.

The doorbell rang, and Richard set his drink aside to greet her. He opened the door to find exactly what he expected. His re-awakened member strained against the bath towel at the sight of her; he did so appreciate a woman who did as she was told. Such a good girl.

"Come inside, Mary."

"Thank you, Richard."

He took the chinchilla coat he'd bought her, sliding the softest material down her arms slowly, rubbing his thumbs across her nipples on the way down.

"I'm so pleased you gave up that hideous bra. This silk dress plays nicely with your delectable figure."

She blushed as if on cue, casting her eyes down and then looking up through her lashes. He hadn't even taught her that; the demure naïveté came naturally to her.

"Thank you, Richard."

She followed him into the living room, where he tossed her coat over the back of the sofa and turned to face her.

Slowly, he assessed the vision in violet silk standing before him. Soft, brown hair freshly washed and brushed, but left to flow naturally over her shoulders, the tips teasing her breasts through thin fabric. He watched with great joy as a shudder passed through her body. She dared not say a word. Good girl.

"Tonight is the night, Mary. You know that, right?"

"Yes, Richard." Her lips trembled in anticipation. She would no doubt enjoy this as much as he. And when they were done with this last test, he would release her into the world to find happiness. Because of him, she would find a man and keep him. He swelled with pride.

Richard took her hand and guided her to the sofa. When she sat, he positioned himself in front of her and gazed upon her glistening, plum lips.

"Mary, you know what to do."

"Yes, Richard. Thank you."

She undid the knot keeping his robe closed, and pushed the lush fabric aside. Taking him into her mouth, Mary worked her magic.

Richard watched her until the sight of him disappearing into her mouth, over and over again, nearly sent him over the edge, despite his prep work. Then he let his head drop back and he relaxed, focusing on the motion she was creating. He let himself feel her soft lips curling as she moved up and down his shaft. Her tongue glided against the underside of him, flicking as she reached the top, softly lapping at the head, then plunging down his length once more, all in one smooth motion. Just like he'd taught her.

Every time she took him back inside her mouth, the motion brought his head to the barrier of her throat and she swallowed lightly, squeezing the tip with every downward stroke. He held on as long as he could, but he'd taught her too well.

An explosion of sensation sent him careening over the edge.

And again, another orgasm hit, this one painful so close on the heels of another. He reached down to shove Mary away, but his hands met empty air.

Richard looked down only to find Mary gone. His pristine apartment, gone. In its place, an infested, filthy hotel room with the front wall completely removed. A dozen or so people stood on an asphalt path, gawking at him as though he were an actor on a stage.

He held himself in his hand and stroked, screaming at himself to stop but helpless to quit the relentless pursuit of another orgasm. And when it came, it felt like knives shooting out of his tip. Tears streamed down his face as he came, again and again.

~*~

How many times will he do that?

Good question, Miss?

Glover. Mrs. Glover.

Well, Mrs. Glover, you see, Richard here was a selfish lover. He lured women in with charm, and bought their trust one gift and compliment at a time. But even those gifts suited his preferences more than theirs. He promised to teach them and, to be fair, he did exactly that. Once he'd trained his *ladies* to be exactly how he wanted them, he had them perform oral sex as a sort of test, and then sent them away.

What an asshole!

Indeed, Mrs. Glover. He believed he was doing something good, though; training lonely women how to please men so they could find and keep one. Richard Bishop seduced and abandoned three hundred and twenty-seven women in such a manner over the course of his lifetime. And so, he will suffer the pain of three hundred and twenty-seven orgasms, repeatedly, for all of eternity.

Well, that's not three hundred and twenty-seven. It's actually an infinite number.

I suppose you're right. Anyone else have any questions? Good. Come along, then. We'll go on through and have our ten-minute period of recovery before we move on to the next enclosure.

~*~

Shut the door behind you, please. Thank you. Now, gather closer but make sure you keep your feet on the green center line.

To your left, you'll see the star of Enclosure Two: Audrey Sinclair. To your right, flickering scenes appear as they do in her mind. An interesting tidbit: even though we stand between her and the scenes, she can see nothing but what she still longs for. In her lifetime, Miss Sinclair often lamented that she didn't have it as good or as easy as others did; was never satisfied with what she did have. She didn't escape that perspective even in death. Her eternity will be spent exactly as her life was: wishing for all the things she was denied. Audrey is perhaps one of the most tragic cases we've seen here at Hell Zoo because her punishment is actually self-imposed.

Now, close your eyes, and open your minds.

~*~

Audrey entered the fast food restaurant through the back door, dropped her purse off in her office to the left, then turned right to join the crew for shift change. The whole time she hopped from the register to the drive-thru window to the warmers, she daydreamed about quitting this shit job and going to work for her dad. One day, he would finally ask her to join him at the store. It was just a hometown furniture store, but she'd been preparing to step in and take over all her life. Well, since she was fourteen, anyway.

She'd enrolled in a business program at trade school and worked in that furniture store throughout her high school and trade school years. When she'd asked about becoming an assistant manager years ago, her dad had told her he didn't need anyone else yet and that she needed supervisory experience anyway. That was why she'd taken the shitty job at a fast food restaurant. She'd climbed the ladder quickly and was biding her time, gaining experience. Now, almost eight years later, she would ask him about it again. Soon. Maybe after Christmas. On the chance he said no, she didn't want a negative note hanging over their holiday celebrations.

Twenty minutes later, the lobby was empty and even the drive-thru traffic had slowed considerably. She escaped the banality of the front end and retreated to her office to call her boyfriend. Some days, he was the only thing that helped her keep her sanity.

"Hello?"

"Hey, Clark. It's Audrey."

"Oh, hey. I'm glad you called. I have something to tell you

and it can't wait."

Her heartbeat sped up. He sounded so serious, and that was either very good or very bad. "Are you sure you want to do this over the phone?"

"Well, I'd rather not, but it can't wait."

He didn't sound excited. He sounded tired or something; Audrey couldn't quite pin down his mood.

"Okay, Clark. What's up?"

"Look, there's no easy way to say this, so I'm just going to say it: I'm seeing someone else."

"You're...wait, what?"

Audrey was emotionally blank. Just completely and totally devoid of any feelings. She shifted into "manager mode" and focused on that. On just having this conversation based on facts. Nothing else. She couldn't handle anything else right now.

"I'm so sorry, Audrey. We never meant for this to happen."

"What do you mean? Wait." They had only been dating a few months. How could he have possibly found someone else so soon? Worse, had he been seeing other women behind her back the whole time? "How long has this been going on?"

"Not long. About a week ago, we were actually shopping for a Christmas gift for you when something happened.

"We kissed.

"And we were both ate up about it, but determined it wouldn't go any further. We met today to discuss what we'd tell you, if we told you at all. It was just a kiss, after all."

She had to force the words through her teeth. "I distinctly hear a *but* coming on..."

"But when we met today..." He paused and Audrey held her breath. What had happened today?

"I can't date you while I'm into someone else. And when I saw her today, I just couldn't pretend I didn't feel anything. That wouldn't be fair to me, and it certainly wouldn't be fair to you."

"Oh, I see. So, you're being fair. To me."

"I know you're pissed—you're entitled. Hate me all you

want, but there is one last thing I have to say to you: stay away from Claire from now on. If you take this out on her, we will get a restraining order. And if you violate that, we will press charges. I want to make that very clear right now."

"What the fuck is wrong with you, Clark? And... Oh, my God. Claire? My best friend, Claire? Really?"

"Get it out now, with me. You won't take this out on her. It's not her fault. It's not anyone's fault, really. You can't help who you're attracted to."

"True enough, but you can choose not to be a dick about it. Why are you treating me like a fucking criminal?"

"Do you hear yourself right now? You're cursing and yelling—"

"I'm pissed! And justifiably so."

"And what happens when you're pissed, Audrey? Hmmm? You remember that time you broke Trisha's nose because she cut your doll's hair off?"

"I was a child. That was completely different!"

"My point stands; you have a bad temper."

"Is that why you wanted to do this over the phone?"

"No, I just didn't want to wait."

"You know I don't hurt people. Aside from that one time Trisha and I fought—and there was a lot more to it than a doll; I ended up with a hairline fracture in my wrist from that same scuffle, but no one seems to remember that—I have never put my hands on anyone."

"The fracture was the result of an accident. You hit Trisha on purpose. Look, that's beside the point—"

"It's exactly the point! God, Clark, it's not bad enough you're leaving me for my best friend, but you make me out to be some kind of abusive monster. What's wrong with you?"

"I'm sorry. I know this is hard for you. Just—everything's going to be okay. It will. You'll move on and find someone who will make you happy. I know you will. It just isn't me."

The line died and she dropped her phone.

Audrey wanted nothing more than to get in her car and drive to the towers. Heights had always soothed her, even in her worst moments. Especially recently, since her mom died.

She swallowed the lump in her throat, and tamped her emotions down when she heard two voices just outside the back door: two teens, barely out of high school.

Beth was on break, but Yvette was due to clock in any minute now. Audrey briefly considered asking the girl to go ahead and clock in, but they all hated her as it was. No use making it worse. It was bad enough she was thirty years old and still working at Mama's Chicken Shack.

Besides, if the girl was late, she'd write her up. Then, at least, she'd have a reason to hate Audrey.

She tried to tune them out, but Yvette's nasally voice grabbed her attention.

"I can't believe that frigid bitch is making us work on Thanksgiving Day."

"I know, right? We'll probably have to work on Christmas, too."

Didn't they understand that someone had to work? She couldn't very well run the place by herself. And she knew good and well that these two weren't doing anything important tonight. Audrey could understand their ire if they had family gatherings to attend, but one of them came from foster parents she hated, a long stint in rehab, and living in a halfway house. And Yvette had a severe aversion to traditions and religion. She'd made it clear she wouldn't be attending any family functions, especially ones that involved Christian holidays. That was the top reason Audrey always scheduled both of them for holidays. It just made sense.

But she was tired of arguing with them, of trying to explain that to the selfish girls. They'd be out of her hair soon enough. With any luck, by January she'd be working in her dad's furniture store.

She closed her office door, not caring whether or not they knew she'd heard them. Her office phone rang just as she was sitting back down.

Her district manager, Jeff, came on the line.

"Hey, Audrey. Glad I caught you. Listen, I want to talk to

you about the supervisor training program coming up. I've got a candidate in your location I'd like you to train."

He spoke so quickly, it left her head spinning.

"Sure, Jeff. Sounds great. Who is it? And–I'm sure they'll ask–where will they go after training?"

"Oh, she'll be taking your place. In fact, I need you at the Monroe location at least four hours every day, starting tomorrow. You can spend eight hours in the afternoons at the Simmesport location training Yvette Sommers. I know the travel will be a pain in the ass, but it's only a week."

Simmesport? Yvette!! The same Yvette that didn't understand why she was the perfect choice to work holidays when almost everyone else had families? The very same one who'd just called her a frigid bitch? Unbelievable.

"Audrey, you still there?"

"Yeah, Jeff. I'm here. Just, trying to work out the logistics. The position in Simmesport, does that come with a raise?"

It damn well better.

"No, it's a lateral move. Anything else? I'm in a hurry. It's Thanksgiving Day."

"Yeah, I'm missing Thanksgiving dinner with my family, too. Is there some kind of relocation bonus? At least mileage reimbursement for making the trip to both locations every day? Something?"

"You know better. If you can't handle it, just say so. I don't have time to argue. The Monroe manager quit without giving notice. Yvette has already been given notice that she's been accepted into the training program, so you'll have to train her to replace you either way. And if you can't make the transition to Monroe, I'll have to find someone else. Someone who doesn't need relocation assistance. No company in this state offers that. It's not even a reasonable request. Jesus.

"Listen, is there anything else pressing that absolutely cannot wait until Monday?"

"But you want me to start on Monday. All of this needs to be settled before then."

"Make a decision Audrey. I've got to go and I won't be

available again until Monday. What's it going to be?"

"I don't have much of a choice, Jeff. You've put me in an impossible position."

"Don't be ridiculous. This is how it works, how it always has. A new hopeful manager applies for the program. If they're accepted, their current manager trains them. Sometimes it's to work at a different location, and if I could move Yvette to Monroe instead, I would, but she has no training."

"But what if I just helped in Monroe temporarily until Yvette's ready to take over? Two weeks, four tops."

"No. I've already told Yvette she can have the Simmesport position."

"Before you spoke to me?"

"I don't answer to you, Audrey. You're walking a fine line."

All the breath whooshed out of her body. Her weak limbs barely able to hold her up, she collapsed into her chair, barely managing to keep her grip on the phone.

"I don't even know what to say. I can't believe you."

"This is business. Same as you scheduling Yvette for every single holiday. She's been complaining about that, you know."

Audrey's face burned and she had to force herself to stop gritting her teeth.

"Not to me. And besides, there's a reason I do that. She doesn't celebrate the holidays. Why would she have a problem with that?"

"I get what you're saying, and that's exactly what I've told her. I have backed you on that point every time she came to me with a complaint because I understand that you're managing a business. Period. And I'm doing the same, just on a much larger scale. I expect you to understand. Do you understand?"

As much as she hated to admit it, she did. That still didn't make it fair. Or right. "I get it."

"Good. So, you'll be in Monroe Monday morning at 5?"

"Seriously?"

"I know it sucks, but you can find a way to make it work. You always do."

With a sigh, she relented. "I'll be there."

"Good. See you soon."

"Yeah, see ya."

"Happy Thanksgiving," he said and hung up.

Thank God it wasn't Christmas. That would have been the worst 'gift' in the history of ever.

Audrey struggled through the rest of her shift, not even bothering to congratulate Yvette on her acceptance into the training program, even though the girl had announced it to everyone as soon as she'd clocked in.

Since the next week would be hell, and because she knew she could get away with it, Audrey juggled a few things and gave herself the rest of the weekend off. Three whole days away from this place. She kind of hope it burned to the ground while she was gone.

Even better if it did so with Yvette trapped inside.

Visions of the young asshole-in-training burning up to a crisp in the Simmesport location accompanied Audrey on the short walk to her car. She cranked up the heater and sat there, fuming.

Yvette was taking her job, Claire had taken her boyfriend. What next? Her sisters taking her dad away from her?

As ridiculous as that sounded, it hit a little too close to home. The twins were terribly spoiled. And because she was nine years older than them, she'd been treated more like the red-headed stepchild from the time they were born than their sibling. It was subtle, but she'd always felt like she was some kind of extra person in their home and, often, something unwanted.

Maybe it was just a culmination of the events of the day, but she distinctly remembered the day the twins came home from the hospital and how it felt. It felt like her parents had been waiting for those two to come along all their lives, and that they didn't quite know what to do with Audrey when they finally got what they wanted.

She forced those thoughts away.

Until she died in June, her mother had repeatedly assured

Audrey that the only reason she ever felt that way was because she'd been the baby–and their only child–for so long, she just didn't want to have to share their attention and affection.

"Everyone struggles with doubt during bad times, hun. I love you. Don't ever doubt that."

Audrey repeated her mother's words now and immediately felt better. On days like today, when those words were all she had, she was intensely grateful for them.

"I love you, Mama," she whispered in the silence. She'd been sitting there with the heat running for so long, she was starting to sweat. So, she turned the heat off, rolled down a window, and pulled out of the lot.

On the way to her apartment–and even later, on the way to her dad's house–she kept thinking about Clark and Claire. She took a small amount of pleasure in knowing their names would look stupid together on the wedding invitations, at least. When sorrow threatened to overwhelm her, she thought about Yvette and Monroe and the weeks ahead of her. Frustration kept depression at bay, and her mental to-do lists brought her right out of her funk.

When she got to her dad's, both her sisters were parked in the driveway. Cammie was parked beside dad, but Trisha– horrible at parking–was taking up too much room behind them for Audrey to be able to fit her car beside her. She'd have to park on the street.

That feeling of being pushed aside, of being squeezed out and not belonging, tried to pull her under again. She wasn't having it. Not tonight.

Audrey parked her car and went inside. A big commotion in the kitchen drew her into the room.

Three pairs of eyes caught sight of her and froze, wide open. Everything was still and quiet for just a beat; then Cammie spoke.

"OMG, Audrey! I'm so happy you're here. I thought you were working?" Cammie bounded over and wrapped Audrey in a hug. "Dad just made an announcement, but he'll make it again. We really didn't think you were going to make it tonight."

She'd never admit it, but Cammie was her favorite. Although they were both spoiled, Trisha had always been so selfish. Cammie had somehow gotten the generosity gene that had skipped her twin altogether.

Audrey loved her sister's enthusiasm.

"I had to work later than I thought I would. But I wouldn't miss seeing you guys on Thanksgiving!"

Cammie smiled warmly and glanced at her dad, prompting him to make his announcement again.

When he flushed a deep red, Audrey knew something was wrong.

"I'm retiring in January, Audrey."

Cammie and Trisha shared wide grins, Cammie practically bouncing in place. Audrey's excitement was on hold, though. Why was he avoiding her gaze?

"Tell her the rest, Dad," Cammie said.

He cleared his throat, stared into his empty cup, and then looked at Cammie.

"Cammie, here, and Trisha are gonna come work at the store."

"Isn't that great?" Cammie and Trisha both looked to Audrey, but she was frozen. Staring at her father. Still waiting for him to meet her eyes.

"Dad?"

Cammie's smile faded abruptly, but where she looked stricken, Trisha looked pissed.

"Let me guess, that's a problem for you," Trisha said. "Really, Audrey? We can't have anything because you want it. I'm guessing you want this, too."

Audrey barely managed a whisper. "I have since I was fourteen years old."

"Oh, great. Even better. Let's see, that would have made me, what? Five years old. But, somehow, I took this from you, didn't I? It's always this way with you. You just can't be happy for me. Ever. At all. It's making the cheer squad all over again. I got in when you never did, and it just about killed you. God,

Audrey, you are so selfish."

Trisha stormed out of the house, but without her keys, purse, or coat. She wasn't going far. Cammie squeezed Audrey's arm.

"We didn't know you wanted to work at the store, Addie."

"It's okay. You couldn't have known. Like she said, you were only five."

"True enough." Cammie looked at their dad uncertainly. "You knew, though. Did you forget?"

"He couldn't have," Audrey answered for him. "Everything I've done since I was fourteen I did so I could work for him."

Cammie seemed about ready to cry. "Dad? Why would you do this?"

"Look, girls, there are things you don't know."

"Obviously," Cammie said. As sweet as she was, she couldn't stand for anyone to hurt her big sister. "I won't work at the store. I won't take the position."

Her dad let out a deep sigh, then fixed himself another drink, speaking over his shoulder as he did.

"Trisha will. She'll be the one to take over the place when I'm gone. Either way is fine, as long as it stays in the family."

For the second time that day, Audrey felt as though she'd had the wind knocked out of her. She couldn't speak; could hardly breathe.

Cammie spoke for her. "What the hell is that supposed to mean?"

"Watch your mouth with me, girl."

Audrey could feel Cammie shaking beside her, and the room spinning around her.

"Your mother and I were told we couldn't have kids. By the time you two came along, we had given up. We'd adopted Audrey nine years before, when she was a baby. She isn't technically my child."

A whole lifetime of insecurities surfaced and swept her legs out from under her. Audrey collapsed.

When she came to, she was alone with Cammie.

"I'm so sorry, Audrey. I can't believe...well, any of it. It's so unfair.

"But just know that you are my sister. Nothing has changed for me."

Audrey tried to accept that, tried to believe it was enough. What had her mother said? She'd been the baby too long, the only child; that was why she felt so out of place. Her mother had always done everything she could to make Audrey believe. Now that she was gone, those words were all Audrey had. And those words were a lie.

She had to get out of there. She didn't know where Dad–or whatever she was supposed to call him now–and Trisha were, but she never wanted to see them again.

"I'm fine, Cammie. I just need some time to process all of this, you know?"

"Sure. Of course. I'll be here when you're ready. I'll always be here for you, Addie. I love you."

"Love you too, Cams."

Audrey started her car, eager to get away from the house where she no longer had any family. Away from the town where she'd been edged out of her job, and far away from the best friend and boyfriend who'd betrayed her.

Her whole life had been taken away from her. There was nothing left. So Audrey sought out the one place where she'd always found peace: the rice drying towers. Some people were afraid of heights, scared to fall. Not Audrey. Looking at the world from a distance had always soothed her.

And tonight, freefalling toward that empty world, rushing toward a blissful end to the emptiness of living, was no exception.

~*~

Audrey Sinclair was a good person surrounded by toxic people who didn't appreciate her, in my humble opinion. At the heart of all her desires, she only ever wanted to be loved. By her parents, by her boyfriend and friend, and even by her co-workers and, later, her employees. And in almost every circumstance, that love was withheld.

Well that's just stupid. Why's she in Hell?

Another good question. And you are?

Casey.

Well, Miss Casey, Audrey is in a self-imposed purgatory. She will continue to relive the events of her life that caused her envy and pain until she lets go. That envy is what holds her prisoner in her own mind. It's understandable, certainly. She only wanted what all beings do: acceptance and unconditional love. It wasn't an unreasonable thing to wish for, and not at all her fault she never received it. But the lack of empathy and compassion turned her into a special sort of sinner, one that will torment herself for how she was treated. As I said, one of the most tragic exhibits of Hell Zoo.

But some part of her *must* know that she is in no way responsible for the actions of others. Maybe it's the romantic in me, but I have hope for her.

Let's move outside and take another breather. I think I speak for all of us when I say we could use it.

~*~

Our next enclosure features a sinner so clichéd as to be downright boring. Nevertheless, let it not be said that Hell Zoo discriminates against anyone at all. If you're ready?

Good. Follow me, please. And stay close. This one is aware of his surroundings and will attack you if he can reach you. It is imperative you remain on the green line while within this particular enclosure.

~*~

"See ya later, Mr. Ackerman."

Hyde waved dismissively, not bothering to acknowledge his trainer's parting courtesy any further than that. He saw the man daily, for Christ's sake. Did they really need to waste time with pleasantries?

He thought not. And if Jim or James or whatever the guy's name was disagreed, that was his problem.

After a quick but thorough shower, Hyde donned his evening attire: a pair of jeans, a crisp white shirt, and a navy cardigan vest. He carefully applied a dab of gel to his hair and used the blow-dryer the gym provided. As he worked, he noticed his cuticles were a bit rough and extended. Making a mental note to get a manicure, he took one last look in the mirror then collected his bags.

Hyde stopped at the dry cleaner to drop off his suits, then detoured a couple of blocks out of his way so he could pick up a bouquet of flowers for Susan. They'd had a bit of a falling out the night before. And even though it wasn't his fault, he still felt compelled to make the gesture. She was his wife, after all, and he did love her.

He just wished she wasn't so flighty. No one needed to move the furniture every time they cleaned a room. And it wasn't like they hadn't had the same conversation before. He thought back to that first time she moved the sofa to the opposite side of the room. Waking in the middle of the night, Hyde had gone to get a sip of water from the kitchen. He had to pass through the living room to get there, and because it was dark, he was sleepy, and she'd moved the sofa, he'd slammed his foot right into the damned thing. Broke his little toe that night.

Susan had heard him yelling and come running down the hall, turning on the lights as she went.

"What happened? Are you okay?"

"Fucking sofa! God damn it, Susan. Why the hell did you move the furniture?"

"It's easier to sweep the floor if I move the sofa, rather than trying to sweep under it."

He managed to stand again, leaning heavily on his uninjured foot.

She hesitated on the other side of the sofa, but when he leaned against the back of it for support, Susan came around with her arms outstretched like she would help him.

A blinding flash of pure rage blacked him out momentarily. When he came around, Susan was kneeling on the floor, pressing a hand to her cheek. His own hand stung. That was the first night he'd had to have what his father called a "heart-to-heart" with her.

"Susan, listen to me."

She sat on her heels, unmoving except for a slight tremble

wracking her entire body.

He gripped her arms tightly and yanked her to her feet. She looked at him then and the terror in her gaze made him sick. Hyde pulled her around the sofa and shoved her onto it, pacing before her.

"I have lived in this house for eight years. I've had countless maids come in to clean at least once a week for those eight years. And can you guess how many times they've moved the furniture to do so?"

Susan stared at the floor, but she managed to answer. "They didn't live here; I do. It's my home, too."

"This is my house! I pay the bills! If anything's broken, I make sure it gets fixed. Not you. This is not your house. You don't make decisions where this house is concerned."

"I could get a job—"

"Why on Earth would you need a job? Is this not enough for you? We have everything we need. And I've made sure you don't want for anything. You even have a shopping budget for clothes every fucking month. What more could you possibly want?"

"That's not what I meant. I just..."

"I don't ask for much, Susan." He took a deep breath, digging for that extra bit of patience. "Just a clean house, a good home-cooked supper every night, and a loving wife. That's all. That's not too much, is it?"

She shook her head no.

"All right, then. Go on back to bed. I'll be there soon."

~*~

As Hyde pulled up under the porte cochére, the bottom of the sky fell out. Instead of continuing across the courtyard and into the garage, he parked there and entered the house through the side entry.

Susan was standing right where she should be: at the stove. She jumped when he opened the door. Must have been lost in thought. Setting down a box of whatever she'd been shaking into the pot, she turned to greet him.

"Hello, Hyde. How was your day?"

Christ, she was like a robot. He was immediately irritated by her stiff posture and automatic conversation. Then he remembered the flowers—saw the reminder of the reason for the flowers on her face—and forced himself to be patient with her. The mornings after they'd had a heart-to-heart were always a bit awkward. And spirited women, his father had told him, always struggled the most with discipline.

He handed her the flowers. Glancing past her into the living room, he noticed the sofa was back where it should be. "It was fine. Same as always, but thank you for asking."

"That's good. Why don't you go on into the living room and relax? I bought you a nice new pair of slippers today."

That was more like it. "Excellent. What's for supper?" he asked as he removed his shoes and brought them to the foyer. He slid his feet into the softest slippers he'd ever felt, and made his way back to his recliner.

"Meat loaf."

His favorite. Finally, Susan was behaving as a woman—as a wife—should. It had only taken him three years to get her trained. Not bad. When they had first met, she was spontaneous and carefree. He had longed to tame that wild heart.

And now it looked like he had. Time would tell.

Hyde lay back in his recliner and drifted off. He woke to a gentle rocking motion.

Susan was gently shaking the chair, not touching him directly, and speaking in a quiet voice so as not to startle him. His last thoughts before sleep took him returned, and he was pleased.

"Supper's ready, Hyde. Are you hungry?"

He smiled at his wife, so close to perfect after only three years. He was damned proud of himself. "Starving," he said as he stood.

She looked happier at his reaction than he thought was strictly normal, but he figured the shift in her mood suited the new and improved Susan.

He followed her to the kitchen, to their bistro-style dining set. Just enough room for two, which was exactly how he liked it. They didn't need extra seating for guests; they never had company over to the house. Any events Hyde hosted were given at the extravagant board rooms at the hotel in the city. His home was his private place, inviolate. And he'd made sure he couldn't have kids long ago. If she ended up pregnant, we'll that would have been cause for a very special heart-to-heart.

Susan set his plate down before him and filled his glass with milk.

They ate in blissful silence. Half-way through his meal, Hyde felt a headache coming on, so he paused to take a couple of ibuprofen.

"Everything okay?" Susan asked.

"Fine," he replied and took his seat again. "Just a headache."

She nodded and went back to her meal.

But as soon as the words were out, Hyde wondered if he wasn't coming down with something. Probably a virus from the gym. He always took antibacterial wipes with him and used them judiciously, but he may have missed something.

A wave of nausea crashed over him, and he gulped down half a glass of milk to soothe the acid burning in his throat.

When his stomach steadied a bit, he continued his meal.

Across the table, Susan moaned.

"Susie?"

She leaned forward, one arm across her middle, tightly holding her stomach.

"Excuse me." She ran out of the room and into the hall bathroom.

He could hear her retching from where he sat. The sounds prompted his own gag reflex. Master bathroom or outside? Kitchen trash was the quickest option, so he emptied the contents of his stomach there.

Glancing down at the chunks of meatloaf, he noticed an alarming shade of red splattering everything.

"What the hell? Susan..."

He crossed the living room and ran down the hall after her,

barging into the small bathroom.

"Susan, what..."

Propped against the wall, Susan sat there, weakly staring at him, with a placid smile on her face. Droplets of blood dotted the otherwise pristine toilet seat and her lips.

"What the hell is wrong with you?"

"Come closer," she whispered.

He knelt down beside her in the cramped space. She reached out with one hand and gripped his shirt as though to pull him in for a kiss.

Considering they'd both been puking, he'd have to pass on this one.

Keeping his mouth a safe distance from hers, he stayed just close enough to hear her.

"Did you know that very few people actually die of rat poisoning?"

"Susan, you're not making any sense. We may have to get you to a doctor."

He hesitated. The bruise on her cheek was still too fresh for her to go out in public. He certainly couldn't bring her to the doctor like that.

Susan coughed and wheezed. Hyde felt short of breath himself. Could it be they'd gotten the same virus? Sweat trickled down the back of his neck.

He tried to pull away from her to get a wet washcloth, but she had a death grip on his shirt.

"You could bleed to death–rat poison does that–but it would take a while. Unless…"

"What? Stop it. Just, try to stay calm. And let go. I need to get up."

Susan punched him in the side! A burning heat plunged into his ribs and it was suddenly even harder to get air.

He put both hands on her shoulders and pushed, using the momentum to lift himself up and away from her.

The warm pain in his side became a sharp, slicing sensation. Then, wetness. In her hand, Susan held a bloody knife.

His shirt was inexplicably sticky.

Hyde stumbled out of the room, cursing the trail of blood he left on the hall carpet as he made his way back to the kitchen. He had to do something...get something to stop the bleeding.

A towel.

Shit. He was just in the bathroom.

Hyde reached for the drawer that held the kitchen linens, but his legs gave out beneath him and he dropped to his knees.

As soon as he hit the floor, he slipped in a puddle of water and fell onto his side.

Not water. Blood. There shouldn't have been so much blood so soon. He was bleeding too fast.

Darkness crept in around the edge of his vision.

~*~

Why isn't he being beaten?

I beg your pardon, Mrs. Glover?

I mean, he's just hanging from strings. None of the others are like that. Why is he...wired like that? Clearly, he was an abusive husband. If this is the hell he must suffer, why isn't he being beaten?

Fair point, but Mr. Ackerman's abuse was never about violence. Not really. It was about control. Do you understand now?

Oh! Okay, that's why he's a *puppet* now. Yeah, I get it. Still...

Mrs. Glover, did you do that?

I don't know what you're talking about.

Mr. Ackerman just hit himself. That's not funny. Ladies and gentlemen, please. This is a dangerous sinner. The wards are here to protect you, but if one of you is somehow reaching past them...

Mr. Spaulding, please don't cross the white line.

I can't stop myself. What's happening? Liam, help me!

Mrs. Glover, you're going to get him killed!

~*~

Police Report

Case No. AK05462218

Date: 14.02.17

Reporting Officer: Michael Jones
Prepared By: Ettie Clark
Incident/Issue: <u>Prohibited paranormal activity, resulting in the death and catatonia of eleven victims. Instigator trapped, but relatively unharmed.</u>
<u>Description of Incident/Issue:</u>
On Tuesday, February 14, 2017, at approximately 1800 hours, Officer Jones was dispatched to a report of unauthorized paranormal activity at Indie City's Hell Zoo, 1302 Parkway Drive. Officers Tandy, Glenn, and Cadet Smith were also dispatched to assist.

"Upon arrival, I observed several staff members of Hell Zoo escorting guests from the premises and a physical makeshift blockade set up at the entrance to (and exit from) the Valentine's Day special exhibit. Cadet Smith and Officer Tandy assisted the staff in evacuating the grounds. Officer Glenn accompanied myself and Hell Zoo's director, Divania Alighieri, into what they called the *Wrathful Lover* enclosure.

"Mrs. Glover (later identified) had apparently crossed a line of sigils and become stuck outside the safe viewing area. Director Alighieri placed a red tracer glow on the threads of magic within the enclosure. One by one, she eliminated the red glow from each thread that was supposed to be there; those from the white lines on either side of the path, those from the neon green line down the center, and those from the sigils above and below the enclosure itself. Even after those lines were removed from sight, glowing red lines remained in abundance. What was left, she explained, were the lines of an unauthorized spell.

"Ms. Alighieri demonstrated an attempt at extraction. To her own magic, she attached a blue tracer glow–much like a contrast injection is used to make blood vessels appear more clearly and in greater detail–so we could watch her work.

"The moment her threads contacted the red threads of the rogue casting, the blue melted into the red, turning the remaining glow purple. The now purple glow spread until all the remaining threads were also purple. For a moment, the threads pulsed collectively. Then pockets of purple gathered at seemingly random points on each line, their color darkening until a new thread burst from each pocket like a popped pimple filled with ethereal tape worms. The new threads uncoiled, effectively strengthening the casting surrounding Mr. Ackerman and Mrs. Glover.

"Mrs. Glover has not been harmed. How long that will remain true is uncertain. For the moment, Mr. Ackerman seems content to control her via the *puppet threads* that had previously controlled him.

"The demonic conduit, Tiba Bato, was shredded by some unknown force. Ms. Alighieri, in a separate statement, alleged that she found no evidence of battle magic residue within the enclosure. Given the state of the three human guides with her, all dead via clearly self-inflicted injuries, it is reasonable to assume that the nightmare demon forced a hallucination upon herself that became her reality. Without the proper wards in place, she was certainly capable. Ms. Alighieri confirms that the thread blocking that specific ability had somehow been removed. When that might have occurred is unclear."

Actions Taken:

"As Ms. Alighieri is currently the most powerful paranormal practitioner known to me, the department will assist her in finding alternate methods for removing Mrs. Glover from Mr. Ackerman's control. The families of the three Hell Zoo staff members have been notified of their deaths. The seven additional guests have all been placed in the care of various county psychiatric hospitals. All attempts to communicate with Tiba Bato beyond the gates of Hell have been unsuccessful. Communication with other demons in Purgatory have turned up no leads on her location, but because we have no way of enforcing laws, they are under no legal obligation to comply. She could very well have made her way back to her home in Purgatory. We have no other way of knowing if her ethereal form survived the incident at all."

Report Summary:

Paranormal tomfoolery leaves four staff members dead–

three guides and one demonic conduit—seven guests catatonic, and one guest trapped in Indie City's Hell Zoo on Valentine's Day, 2017. Sole survivor is Mrs. Alice B. Glover, still trapped within the *Wrathful Love* enclosure of Hell Zoo's special Valentine's Day exhibit at the time of this report. Attempts by the staff of Hell Zoo to free Mrs. Glover have resulted in an unusual contamination of the wards already in place, making a rescue more difficult, if not impossible. Nightmare demon Tiba Bato's ethereal form is assumed at large.

~*~

Angel's Catch
Daniel Arthur Smith

~*~

Jack and Jill went up the hill to fetch a pail of water. The drought in the glen had been ceaseless. Three full seasons of dust fields and parched earth. Their destination was the puddle of a pool called Angel's Catch, the fount of a mountain spring that ran so sparse, the precious water evaporated long before making its way down the hillside. Old Dame Dob had promised the village that the blessed hilltop water would seed the well that had nearly run dry, that the rains would follow the water of the Angel's Catch and bring back a season of flush prosperity, but only on the condition that the glen's first son and first daughter made the two-day ascent. So it was that Jackin, heir to the King, and Jillian, daughter of the village's wealthiest family, were sent forth. They were the same age– Jack and Jill–both due to take rites the next solstice. That Jill had eyes for the Baker's son was no secret to Jack. He kept his interest hidden. Old Dame Dob had changed everything.

They were on the second day of their quest, and Jill had not spoken or met eyes with Jack since they awoke. This troubled him. He felt it far unfair. The night before, they'd stayed in the hovel at Paradise Landing. If a place were ever misnamed, it was that pile of rocks and the planked roof lean-to sprouting from it. Even with a small fire, the open aired shelter was brutally cold. In an effort to keep warm, they'd agreed to hold each other close through the night. They were talking then. Jill had asked him why the pool was called the Angel's Catch. He supposed it was because the pool was so high up the mountain. He asked if she believed the drought would end when they brought the water down to the glen, and she said she did. Then they both agreed that they would be heroes and that songs would be sung. And after that, he buried his face deep into her sweet-smelling auburn hair and went to sleep. Nothing else happened. He was honorable, her virtue undisturbed, but this morning, for no reason apparent to him, she went quiet.

Again this day, Jack carried the supplies and buckets as his burden. Jill had teased that the shoulder yoke contrasted with his crown. The teasing didn't bother him. The joyful humor was far preferable to the silence. Silence made the journey more miserable. He trudged behind, gazing at the purple stalks of dry heather parted from the path by the long hem of Jill's tartan dress. Then he studied her dress, and she within it, the locks of auburn hair that flowed to her thin waist, so perfectly bright that the light of the horizon glowed through. It was as if she wore a fiery crown.

His thoughts drifted back to their night and how he had nuzzled into her, the delicious smell of her hair.

Jack caught himself, and shook his head clear. Who was he to puzzle about her anyway? No man could figure a girl. He put his gaze beyond her, toward the high hill horizon. Neither had made the journey before. Few had. But by verse they were prepared for what they would find at the mountain top, a lone rowan tree, and at its base, *allt aingeal glac*—the Angel's Catch. From either side of his shoulder yoke, an empty bucket hung. He was to fill one bucket on their evening arrival and the other on the morning departure. This drew him to ponder the trip back down to the glen. His legs were already tired, and it was only midday. The monotony made the ache worse.

Hours passed. Finally, Jack decided he could stand the

silence no more.

"Are we going to stop?" he asked.

Jill continued climbing without response.

"I'm getting hungry," he added.

This time she answered, "We're almost there. I can see it."

Jack squinted at the horizon; nothing had changed. Before them was the endless field of heather, but then, with his next step, he saw it, shades lighter than the field: the fuchsia top of the flowering rowan tree. With each step, more of the tree lay bare.

When Jill reached the top of the ridge, she stopped to wait for Jack.

In awe, Jill blankly said, "Would you look at that."

"Aye," he replied.

Neither were prepared for what they'd found: a misty, bottomless void just over the other side of the hill. Rooted in an overlooking crag, the flowering rowan. Slowly, they made their way to it. Sure enough, at the tree's base was a small pool, the Angel's Catch, and flowing from it, cut into the mountain rock, a trickle of a stream that dripped down into the abyss.

"We should make camp," said Jill.

"Yes. But first let's do our duty and fill the bucket."

"Okay. Right. That's a good idea."

Jack dropped the yoke from his shoulders, knelt down, and dipped the bucket into the clear water. "Dame Dob was right," he said. "There's not enough water for two. We'll draw one now and then the other before we leave in the morning."

As he pulled the full bucket away, a web of lightning flashed across the sky. Followed by the high rumbling roar of thunder.

Wide eyed, they both looked to the angry sky.

"Is this it?" asked Jill. "The reckoning we've been waiting for?"

"I believe so. After three dry seasons, the sky will finally share her wealth of rain. Let's make camp."

It was warmer on this side of the mountain. Moist heat rose from the abyss. Still, it was damp, so Jack gathered what fallen twigs and branches he could find around the tree's bottom and built a fire. For the most part, Jill remained quiet, but her mood was better. As Jack relaxed, his mind spun back to a green glen, as it had been before the draught. They were going to be heroes, but more importantly, they were going to save the village.

When Jack awoke, Jillian was already cooking breakfast on the fire. The sky was dark, filled with thick pillowed storm clouds that intermittently glowed red and white from within. The flowers in the rowan above that had been a mild fuchsia yesterday had become a deep scarlet. Jack blinked to refocus. It seemed that all of the colors around him were more defined: the ebony and blue marbled into the rocks around the pool; the browns and greens of the dried grasses; and the pinks of the heather on the ridge. Even the orange of the fire. But what stuck out the most to him was Jill's brightly glowing auburn hair and ivory skin.

"I don't remember going to sleep," Jack said.

Jill smiled and said, "It was the trek up the mountain took its toll. You sat and your lights went with you."

"Yeah, I s'pose. I was quite laggard toward the end." He stood and stretched his arms high above his head, then walked around the side of the rowan tree. "I don't think there's enough water in the Catch," he said.

"What's that?"

"There's not enough to fill the second bucket."

Jill moved the small cakes from the fire and then stood to join him. She crossed her arms. "Old Dame Dob told me this might happen. She gave me something that will help."

"What charm did she give you?"

"No charm." Jill slid a hand into the deep hidden pocket of her dress and pulled out a folded piece of parchment. "It's this note she gave me. I'm to read it."

"A note? How is that going to help?"

"I believe it's a thank you note to the Angels of the pool. She told me that I was to read the note aloud and then…"

"And then what?"

"And then I was to be married."

"So that's what the cold face was all about. Well, don't worry. I won't hold you to it."

"You don't have to. Hold me to it I mean."

"I know about Alastair."

"Alastair? What could you possibly mean?"

"The baker's son? C'mon. Everyone knows that you two have been sneaking about, making plans."

Jill scrunched her face. "Ah. Are there no secrets in the glen?" she said. "I assure you there's nothing particular with Alastair Boyd. I simply meant that you don't have to hold me to it on your part. There must be someone that you're already in love with."

"There is."

"There is?"

"Yes."

"It's Megan isn't it. I see the way she looks at you. She can't wait to be princess."

"No. It's not Megan."

"Abigail?"

Jack shook his head.

"Edna?"

"No."

"Well who then?"

Jack placed a hand on either side of her waist. "You, Jill. You're the girl of my heart. I've been in love with you since we were children."

Jill's ivory cheeks went rosy and her head bowed down. In a soft voice she asked, "Then you'll have me?"

"I couldn't be happier. What about Alastair?"

"You and the whole glen let your minds wander too much. I help him with his studies. That's all."

"His studies?"

"The boy can't do math. It's a wonder he can make bread, much less take over his father's business. Let me read this note so that more water will come."

Jill took Jack's hand into hers and let her arm stretch out.

Their fingers mingled then slipped away, as she walked to the edge of the crag. She unfolded the yellow paper Dame Dob had given her and read the words inked upon it. Jack did not understand all that she said–the language was the old tongue– but he was sure that the spirits understood every thick syllable. The branches of the rowan tree above rustled, as if the limbs were awakening. Again, lightning webbed across the sky, accompanied by the loud roar of thunder.

At his feet, the pool began to fill. "It's working," he said, dropping to his knees, a grin wide across his face. They were going to be heroes and he was to have a new bride, the most beautiful girl in the glen.

The Angel's Catch rapidly filled to the point that the overflow ran into the crack of a stream, and trickled down from the cliff into the abyss. Instantly, a mist began to rise beyond the crag.

Each of Jill's words invited more lightning and thunder, until the sky of black clouds glowed so red, it appeared to Jack that a fire burned in the firmament above.

The red of the cloud fire spread to the horizon, where the mist of the abyss and clouds met, working its way into the void below, growing in brightness until the mist before them glowed ember red.

A familiar pat came upon Jack's head, followed by another, and then another. He reached up to rub the wet in his hair. Blotches of rain water collected upon the toe stones surrounding the pool. "What spell is this?" Jack whispered, while at the tip of the cliff, Jill competed with the thunder, slowly shouting out the old poem, enunciating every syllable as a declaration.

The fat drops grew in number as the skies released their burden. Jack found himself in a downpour of glorious fresh water. He held his arms out and up to embrace the rains, and then turned his attention back to Jill.

Before her, a shadow was forming in the boiling wall of light and mist. The silhouette spread wide into, "Wings," said Jack. For that's what they were: the huge wide spread wings of a bat…no… Abruptly, Jack screamed, "Stop! Stop! You've summoned a dragon!"

Jill moved back, away from the cliff. She turned to Jack and he grabbed her hand, and pulled her behind as his feet dug deeply into the hill.

The rain had become more forceful, missiles of water darting from the new gusts. Jack leaned forward and pulled hard. "We have to move quick," he said. "Get over the ridge before it sees us."

"We have to take the buckets!" yelled Jill.

"There's no time!" said Jack. "If we don't make it to the ridge, we'll be slaughtered."

With each step, the wind became fiercer and the ground less sure. His shoes slid upon the husks of the dead drenched grasses and the slick of the hillside mud.

"We have to take the buckets!" Jill repeated. "Or the rains will stop."

"What are you talking about?"

"Dame Dob said the rains follow the water of the Angel's Catch!"

Jack looked back. The glowing clouds of the sky and abyss had merged. The boiling mass rolled in close, furling into the highest limbs of the rowan. And there, looming above the sacred tree, the silhouette of the red dragon, directly above the yoke and buckets.

"Keep going!" yelled Jack. He flung himself over onto his back. The beast was close and he feared he would see it break through the thin veil mist.

Jack raised himself from the cold wet ground, but before he could stand, his feet slipped beneath him and with a splat he fell back on his behind. His blood pumped hard. With a thud, he dug each heal into the hillside, then laboriously he lifted himself again, slowly, until he stood. With weight on one foot he stepped the other forward, and almost immediately dropped again. He caught himself. His shoes would not grip. It was only a short distance to the yoke. A few more steps and he'd have it. Jack sucked in a deep breath and ran forward. By moving rapidly, he thought, he would cheat a fall—and the dragon. He was focused on his prize…but the rain was so loud, he didn't hear Jill shriek out from behind as she slid uncontrollably down the hill and was caught by surprise as she crashed into him. The blow threw him forward, into the rowan. Jack fell down, and broke his crown, and Jill came tumbling after.

Unable to stand, Jack scurried on his knees toward her.

But it was too late. Before Jill could let a word escape, tentacles reached out of the mist and embraced her.

"No!" Jack screamed as Jill, entangled in the red tentacles of the dragon, was lifted from the cliff and pulled into the cloud.

He could only watch the dark of the massive wings flap away into the deep red glow, leaving him alone.

The rain persisted, but the wind died down. The dragon and Jill were gone. He inspected his broken crown. Too bent to wear, he placed it into his pack, and then loaded himself with his burden. Carefully and slowly he climbed to the ridge and began his journey down the other side. And when he reached Paradise Landing, he relit the fire he'd built on the journey upward, and then recalled the old woman's words. He did not fear the dragon would come for him. He lay in the spot where he had nuzzled Jill, imaging her and her fresh smelling hair. He understood all too well what Old Dame Dob had meant. *Allt aingeal glac*–the Angel's Catch–was not named for the water collected in the spring. It was named for what took place there. Jill was never to be married to him. It was the place maidens were given to dark Angels to take as their brides in return for the rains.

~*~

ABOUT THE AUTHORS

S. Elliot Brandis is an engineer and author from Brisbane, Australia. He writes post-apocalyptic and dystopian fiction, often infused with a variety of outside elements. He is a lover of beer, baseball, and science fiction.

His novels are about outlaws, outcasts, and outsiders.

For more information, visit selliotbrandis.com

Nathan M. Beauchamp started writing stories at nine years old and never stopped. From his first grisly tales about carnivorous catfish, mole detectives, and cyborg housecats, his interests have always delved into strange waters. Nathan works in finance so that he can support his habit of putting words together in the hope that someone will read them. His hobbies include reading, photography, arguing for sport, and pondering the eventual heat death of the universe. He has published many short stories in magazines and anthologies, and holds an MFA in creative writing from Western State. He lives in Colorado with his wife and two young boys. Nathan co-created the award winning YA science fiction series **Universe Eventual** where he writes as N.J. Tanger. The series includes *Chimera*, *Helios*, and *Ceres* and the prequel *Ascension*. **Universe Eventual** is available on Amazon.

For more information, visit njtanger.com

Will Swardstrom is a speculative fiction author. His latest novel is *Blink*, the first adventure in *The Utility Company* series, co-written with his brother Paul. He also has two full length novels, *Dead Sleep* and *Dead Sight*, and is at work on the finale in the trilogy. He also has three stories in The Future Chronicles anthology series (*Uncle Allen* in *The Alien Chronicles*, *Z Ball* in *The Z Chronicles*, and *The Control* in *The Immortality Chronicles*). Each of those anthologies has charted in the Top 5 on the SF Anthology list and The Alien Chronicles reached as high as #6 on the Overall Top 100 List. The Control from The Immortality Chronicles has been nominated for Best American Science Fiction. He also has a few stories set in Hugh Howey's WOOL Universe among his various other short stories and novellas. He lives in Southern Illinois with his wife and two kids.

For more information, visit
willswardstrom.wordpress.com

Hester J. Rook is an Australian writer and co-editor of **Twisted Moon** magazine, a magazine of speculative erotic poetry (http://twistedmoonmag.com). She has previous prose and poetry publications in **Strange Horizons**, **Apex Magazine**, **Liminality Magazine**, **Strangelet** and others. Visit her on Twittter @kitemonster.

Kevin Lauderdale has written essays and articles for the *Los Angeles Times*, *The Dictionary of American Biography*, and **McSweeneys.net**. His short fiction has appeared in several of Pocket Books' *Star Trek* anthologies as well as various small press publications. His story "Box 27" appeared in the science journal *Nature*. This is his second James and Reggie story for Canyons of the Damned. His story "James and the Dark Grimoire," which made Ellen Datlow's Honorable Mention list for the year's best horror and was nominated for a Washington Area Science Fiction Association Small Press Award for Best Short Story was reprinted in *Canyons* #6. More James and Reggie adventures are in the Canyons pipeline. With Jeff Ayers, he has written *The Fourth Lion*, a YA thriller set in contemporary Washington, D.C. and its surroundings. He hosts the Old Time Radio podcast, *"Presenting the Transcription Feature,"* and co-hosts *"Temple of Bad,"* the podcast about movies that are so bad, they're practically a religious experience, both on the Chronic Rift network. He is a member of SFWA and HWA.

Jessica West (a.k.a. West1Jess) is currently pursuing a state of self-induced psychosis, also known as writing. In the past, she has worked for Wal-Mart, a lawyer, and a bank. Now if she could just get a couple years experience with the IRS and the NSA, world domination is in the bag.

Jess lives in Acadiana with three daughters still young enough to think she's cool and a husband who knows better but likes her anyway.

Daniel Arthur Smith is the author of the international bestsellers *Hugh Howey Lives*, *The Cathari Treasure*, *The Somali Deception*, and a few other novels and short stories. He also curates the phenomenal short fiction series *Tales from the Canyons of the Damned*.

He was raised in Michigan and graduated from Western Michigan University where he studied philosophy, with focus on cognitive science, meta-physics, and comparative religion. He began his career as a bartender, barista, poetry house proprietor, teacher, and then became a technologist and futurist for the Fortune 100 across the Americas and Europe.

Daniel has traveled to over 300 cities in 22 countries, residing in Los Angeles, Kalamazoo, Prague, Crete, and now writes in Manhattan where he lives with his wife and young sons.

For more information, visit danielarthursmith.com

~*~